VICIOUS REDEMPTION

FIVE DARK FANTASIES

MICHAEL WARREN LUCAS

Tilted Windmill Press

COPYRIGHT INFORMATION

Wednesday's Seagulls: Originally published on "short-story-me Genre Fiction," August 2010.

Pax Canina: Previously unpublished

Opening the Eye: Originally published in "Horror Library, volume 2," Cutting Block Press, 2007

Breaking the Circle: Originally published in "Women who Run with the Werewolves," Cleis Press, 1996.

Sticky Notes: Previously unpublished.

FOR LIZ

WEDNESDAY'S SEAGULLS

I'd dry-swallowed the last instant coffee days ago, but the thought "Oversleep and he'll eat your brain" gutkicks you awake. No matter how tired you are. Two or three nights with only a couple of hours sleep puts sand in your brain and smothers your joy in life. Six nights like that, and your brain glues shut and your energy dwindles into bovine endurance just this side of death.

I spasmed awake at the first flicker of dawn. When I saw that enough tide remained to leave a ribbon of saltwater between Wednesday and myself, I released my breath and massaged crud from my eyes. Nothing had changed. A hundred-foot rock in the middle of the South Pacific. The shattered plane I slept in. And the dead man, Wednesday.

Wednesday stood so still the island danced in comparison. Sunlight glinted off the golden hoop dangling from the desiccated stub of his left ear. His right leg ended in twin spears of worm-eaten brown bone. Salty air coursed through the crack in his skull and out his broken teeth, whistling loudly enough to penetrate the crash of the ocean's fierce churn around us, and the corrugated tear across his gut displayed mummified bowels and stumps of rib. I couldn't imagine how long he'd been on this rock – years? Centuries? How long did it take to turn a human being into jerky, and how long could human jerky last? Six bullets had lodged harmlessly somewhere inside him, and the flare gun hadn't singed his petrified invulnerability.

Only paces behind Wednesday, the island's west end rose in a flattened dome of broken rock. Hundreds of seagulls wheeled overhead, and the rising sun flickered on the waves, but nothing else moved. The sky mirrored the ocean, diffusing the horizon. Traditionally a castaway gets a single coconut tree, but I'd been shorted even that. Robinson Crusoe even got a native to help him live like a civilized man. I'd called mine Man Wednesday, as he was obviously a couple days short of a Man Friday. It had seemed funny, the first day. Everything had seemed funny that first impossible day, but the endless days bludgeoned surrealism into blunt reality.

If I could survive long enough to be rescued, it would be on seagulls and plane wreckage alone.

I forced myself to relax, leaning against a spire of rock and cradling the strut I'd finally pried out of the wreckage. The strut had felt solid and invincible when I'd been pounding and prying and scraping at the bolts holding it to the wing over the past few days. Now it felt too frail to support the hope I had for it. I'd had a much better shaft the first day, solid steel an inch thick and two feet long. I'd tried to crack Wednesday's skull the rest of the way open. He'd raised an arm to block it, and the impact of the bar against his exposed bone was like hitting a light post. The shock had stunned my grip open and I let the shaft bounce deep into the churning water. That was when I realized that if Wednesday came close enough to grab me, I was dead.

The cuts and tears lining my palms and fingers weren't painful compared to how the rest of me felt.

The receding tide had almost erased the moat when a seagull landed on Wednesday's shoulder and tentatively pecked at a tangle of human jerky. Wednesday resisted as much as any other piece of garbage, so the bird sank his beak into a tricep and flapped to tear it free. Rattlesnake-quick, faster than I could follow, a skeletal hand lashed up and seized a wing. The bird screeched and thrashed, but in moments Wednesday had gnawed open its skull and scraped out the runny gray insides with his ragged tongue. I had thought brain-eating zombies were just in the movies, but once again he dropped the hollowheaded carcass at his feet.

When Wednesday finished eating the tide had fallen enough that he could totter towards me without getting wet, the bones in his right leg skewing around each other with every step. I staggered a wide circle around him, skirting the north edge of the island, then slowed so he could trail only a few yards behind.

The island's west end jaggedly plateaued ten feet or so above the low-tide line, cracked by exposure into a three-dimensional jigsaw with countless handholds and ledges. Kids would love climbing that slope, but six nights of scattered sleep weakened my grip and scratched my vision. Each step was an act of will. The strut clenched in my armpit made me a little more clumsy, but I'd circled this rock every fifteen minutes, eighteen hours a day, for days now, and my hands and feet knew the best route without troubling my exhausted brain. I clambered a few yards across the rock until I hit the spot where two small stone shelves cradled my heels a foot above the crashing water and I could rest my buttocks on the slope.

Wednesday's sunken eyes studied me, then he stumbled into pursuit just as he had every other time. Stump leg flapping uselessly, he dragged himself across the slope with his hands and used the remaining leg as a brace. His fingernails, brown as gnawed tombstones, did not break no matter how fiercely he clawed the stone. He needed almost two minutes to haul himself to within five feet of me. The first day I'd learned that if I got more than twenty feet ahead he circled around the other way, which made his stumpy leg almost useful. If I let him come too close, he'd use those cadaverous teeth on my head.

He never stopped following. *Never.* No matter how I begged, or screamed, or prayed. Without the twice-daily high tide to put six feet of uncrossable water between us for a couple precious hours of sleep twice a day, I would have been dead a week ago. I'd tried bashing in his head with a steel bar. I'd tried a lasso, and a tripline. I'd rigged the plane's battery and salvaged wire into an electrical trap that would have knocked me out. He couldn't be crushed, he couldn't be tied up, and electric shock hadn't even raised the few ghastly strands of hair left on his head. I was down to sticks and stones – and on this rock, I had to provide my own stick.

Halfway around the island, instead of resting I threw the strut on top of the rock and pulled myself up after it. Usually I'd follow the easier route near the water, but this turgid chase would end today. It had to end today. I didn't have the strength to try anything else.

Fractures and crevices covered the summit, and I quickly wedged my strut into the crack I'd selected days ago. With Wednesday out of sight I only wanted to rest, but I leaned into the lever instead. Cadaverous hands clenched the edge as I felt the crevice groan, and a rock about my size might have shifted underfoot. I caught two deep desperate breaths before Wednesday's head appeared. Once he started hauling himself up, I dropped down the other side.

I veered from the loop to snatch the decapitated seagull. If I didn't have a zombie after me I could catch my own seagulls, but until then I'd live on Wednesday's leavings. For the last three days, I'd used most of these precious minutes to pound and scrape at the bolts holding the strut in place; a few moments to simply breathe felt almost like a vacation. My hands plucked as I waited, spiny feathers inflaming my savaged hands.

When Wednesday shambled into view around the rock I took a deep breath, waiting for him to come close enough that I could trot around him and make him scuttle all the way back to the rock, treasuring every minute I could to try to rest.

First trip of the day, finished. Dozens more to go.

On the sixth circuit I finished plucking and used my pocketknife's last remaining blade to scrape out the bowels, then spread the carcass on the wreck's south wing for what cooking the sun provided. My mouth tightened at the thought of an evening spent perched on the wrecked plane devouring that juicy pink flesh, only faintly grilled by the sun-heated wing, watching Wednesday shuffle back and forth, frustrated by six feet of thigh-deep salt water. Seagull and a couple pints of collected rain water would hold me together for another day.

Then I went back to heaving at the rock. My head spun and my guts burned, but I pushed for a panicked few moments every time we circled the rock. My twelfth session, the rock creaked and left a finger-wide gap behind it. I left the remaining skin from my right knee behind in payment, stumbling and swearing until the sting stopped.

A brief rain shower interrupted me on my twenty-second trip around the rock. Wednesday kept after me, but with the slope too slippery to ascend I contented myself with following the easier path around the shoreline, soaking up water in my shirt and licking it from crevices in the rock. I lost track of how many times we went around before the rain stopped, the sun dried the rocks, and I could climb back up again.

During my twenty-ninth stint at the prybar, the rock shifted far enough that I could thrust a fist into the gap. Finally, on the thirty-first circuit, the boulder groaned and lurched free, shifting a vital few degrees towards the edge. I held my breath, afraid a scream of hope and frustration and would drive the rock over the edge and into the water. When the rock balanced and held still, my laugh sounded more like a harsh croak. For once, I felt like telling Wednesday to hurry up.

The next pass around I took the lower, easier path rather than climbing to the summit. That route had the best resting spot, a smooth patch some three feet wide with a gentle pitch towards the ocean. My boulder now loomed over it. I jammed my abused hands flat against my legs to force my fingers straight, grimacing, waiting.

Wednesday dragged along my trail, the stump of his right leg flailing uselessly over the water. His hip scraped with each lurch. Five feet away, the grind of dead flesh against rock drowned out the ocean's constant splash, and I smothered an urge to bolt. I'd never let Wednesday come this close before, but I needed his feet on the very spot I stood. A bright slice of blue ocean shone through his cracked skull and out his mouth.

One bony hand gripped an outcropping a foot from my head and I leaped, seizing a ledge beside the loosened boulder and blowing out air as I dragged myself up. I imagined those withered claws snatching my legs, and I kicked frantically as I clawed and jackknifed my weight, not even slowing as my fingernails ripped from their beds. Wednesday's hands scuttled below as I knelt beside my teetering rock, only a few feet above him. In less than a minute he'd find a way up, or decide to go around. I wedged the strut tightly against the rock and heaved.

The boulder groaned against its parent rock, immobile. I suddenly thought that I'd been wrong, that this chunk of rock was actually the tip of an spire rooted deep below, it wasn't actually detached and I was trying to split raw stone with my puny lever. I pulled even harder. Wednesday shuffled back and forth underneath, almost ready to circle around to an easier slope.

The boulder shifted a foot, and the strut screeched into a curve. I threw my feet against the freshly-exposed stone, braced my back against another rock, and straightened my legs. The boulder lurched away from the plateau and balanced, wobbling, as if considering falling back towards me. With a wordless snarl I shoved harder. I tasted thick blood, pain fluorescing in my back and panic in my brain, then gravity snatched the boulder and yanked it down. The thunderous crash wasn't as harsh as its echo through the rock.

I lay motionless, trying to make my lungs stop heaving and my empty bowels unclench. Even the thought that I'd missed, that Wednesday was climbing after me, didn't give me strength to move for another dozen breaths. I finally dragged my legs under me and shuffled painfully to peer down.

The boulder had nailed Wednesday, pinning his legs and lower torso. He'd stopped sliding short of the tide line, but the way his arms flailed at the boulder proved he couldn't get enough leverage to move. My head drooped over the outcropping, eyes glazing, then I rolled onto my back and painfully sucked air for a few minutes before allowing myself a bloody-toothed smile. I idly wondered if I'd mention Wednesday to whomever found me.

I awoke in that spot at sunrise with fresh seagull shit on my chest, a new layer of sunburn, and my brain where I'd left it. Every joint felt full of ground glass, and my nose and mouth burned. I'd never been happier. Below me, Wednesday still flailed at the boulder, possibly just a little less quickly. Seagulls had soiled my dinner, so I chucked the carcass into the ocean and promised myself fresh poultry that evening.

Weakness had replaced hunger, so I worked slowly and cautiously. Favoring my sprained back and endless contusions I assembled scraps of twisted metal and fabric into a dark SOS against the shiny fuselage. By noon, a plastic bag became a funnel to guide more rainwater down the wings into a makeshift bucket, and I found nine salt-damp gumdrops between the seat cushions. My white shirt became a distress flag. A soapless saltwater bath in a still tidal pool deliciously scoured days of sweat and filth from my skin. When the rain came I lay on my back and laughed as fresh water burned my sunburn and gnawed lips.

Seagulls whirled overhead. I hurled a fist-sized rock at one.

I missed.

Seagulls were harder to catch than I had thought. They dodged thrown rocks, not that I had many to throw. A sharp twist of fuselage became a spear, but they fluttered away before I came close enough to stab. If I stood still they approached, but never close enough to seize. The screaming rush with outstretched hands didn't work at all.

My checks on Wednesday assumed new intensity. If he grew resigned and stopped thrashing, gulls would approach him. Surely I could spear a *decapitated* seagull from beyond his reach! His movements slowed, but grew no less constant. Surrounded by blue water mirroring the sky, with no horizon between the two, I felt suspended in an endless waste. Weak swallows of precious rainwater couldn't drown the tastes of rancid gumdrop or seat padding. I began wondering if I could slice chunks off Wednesday, or was his flesh too pickled by age and salt to chew? Forget cannibalism; was "dead man walking" contagious?

I tried fishing, standing in the ocean two feet from the shore but up to my waist, sheltered from the ocean current by the rock itself. My line was thread from the seat, the hook a twist of wire. Fish don't bite on seat cushion. I managed to seize a few the tiny minnows in the tidal pool, but the starfish I chewed up had me doubled around my gut in pain for an afternoon.

Days passed. Maybe a week. My body felt as if it belonged to someone else and I just sat behind the eyes occasionally pulling levers. Sweet, luscious gull meat filled my dreams. I heaved chunks of broken engine at the sky and fashioned baitless traps from wreckage. Succulent seagull taunted me from just out of reach. Soon, I would be just as sun-dried as Wednesday. Unable to escape or eat, Wednesday would eventually lie still in real death.

Too little sleep is better than the long sleep. I had spent an agonizing day trapping Wednesday, but pushing that rock off him and into the ocean only took three minutes.

PAX CANINA

On the nights I come home furious, I can't get to sleep without running six or seven miles. My brother Eric says that jogging through my run-down neighborhood at midnight isn't a good idea, but I've never had any trouble. My ratty old sweatsuit and battered sneakers show muggers I'm not worth the trouble, and I'm too big to hassle for kicks. I ignored the bleak November sky and ran down the street.

Doctor Haldeman always wasted his own time, but he'd never wasted mine before. I'm just an emergency room housekeeper, but the thought of him putting his bloated ego in front of a patient's pain infuriated me, driving my feet faster. I didn't slow down until I crossed the train tracks, three miles from home.

A mile later I stopped and shook my arms and neck. In all my limbs, the muscle knots had softened to aches. Each breath of cold air chilled my throat. The churning clouds overhead gleamed with the reflected streetlights. When I turned around, lightning flickered on the horizon. I thought I might get home before the thunderstorm hit, if I hurried. I like rain, but a November thunderstorm in Detroit is colder than a blizzard.

About halfway home, the first cold bombs of rain hit my hair and clothes. My clothes became colder and wetter, and I began fantasizing about hot showers and crisp sheets. Even the growing thunder didn't wake me.

I was only three blocks from home when a motor's sudden roar startled me. I turned towards the road just in time to see an old pickup surge forward and swerve across the center line. Abrupt highbeams silhouetted a low shape that bounced off the truck's bumper and hurtled into the air. The stark light made the scatter of blood look like black rain falling sideways. Someone laughed. I heard the truck accelerate as the body bounced on the sidewalk twenty feet in front of me.

The taillights were already receding as I dashed forward. The flying shape had been a dog, wearing a thin leather collar. Either the truck or the sidewalk had broken its back, slamming its hips against its head. Rib shrapnel punctured the white fur. Mucus and blood drooled from its mouth and ear and puddled with the rainwater.

Lightning burned the sky, close enough to pull at my wet hair. Thunder followed half a heartbeat later.

The dog quivered when I touched its head. My rage blossomed again, richer than when I had left work. I fought death every day, and people just made more. They went out of their way to make more. I wanted to run after the truck, belt the driver, fire a few shots after it, anything to vent that thick passion.

The dog struggled for a breath, then another; then it shuddered and stopped moving. Lightning came again, so close that I heard the thunder simultaneously and my hair rose despite the water matting it down. The flash bleached the dog's bloody fur white.

I checked the tags on the collar. The dog had belonged to Mrs. Frubacher. The spidery old lady walked past my house every day with a cane in one hand and the elderly terrier's stretched leash in the other. I hadn't recognized the dog in the dark rain.

Gritting my teeth, I stripped off my wet sweatshirt. Rainwater and blood slicked the dog's fur as I tried to sling the shirt under it. The November storm drenched my T-shirt, but anger kept me from freezing. When I lifted the body, I smelled blood and emptying bowels even through the drowning rain. Lightning made the world white again.

I stood in the rain and rang Mrs. Frubacher's doorbell for five minutes before the porch light came on. She scowled fiercely as she swung the inner door open, but her face crumpled when she saw her dog dripping through my sweatshirt. "Oh, my God," she said, throwing the screen door open. "What happened?"

"Someone ran him over out on Eleven Mile."

"Oh, no, no." Tears already streamed down her leathery face as she reached for the dog's head. The wet wind rustled her robe, and another flash of lightning cut her face into slivered shadows. "Who did it?"

My stomach burned. "I don't know. The bastard aimed; he hit him for kicks." I knew I should speak more gently, but I couldn't.

Mrs. Frubacher caressed the dog's muzzle with her bony hand. "Oh, Sparky. Why'd you get out?" Her hand trembled, then her whole body shook.

Exhaustion made everything except my anger and her misery feel very distant. "You want to take the body to a vet tomorrow?"

She shook her head. "I won't have him cremated, I want him here, I want him in the garden." She looked at me with silvery eyes. "Would you help me bury Sparky, Mr. Keith?"

Great. "Sure."

She touched my bare arm with her bloody hand, then guided me down the driveway.

We picked a spot in the flowerbed by the back door. She showed me the shovel, and I dug. Any old lady who has trouble using a trowel to plant flowers can't dig a grave for a twenty-pound dog. The first shovelful of wet dirt made my back burn in complaint. The second wasn't any better.

"He was such a good dog, you know," she said. "He kept me company, he listened to me. He cared. People say that dogs don't have feelings, but Sparky did." The rain had matted Mrs. Frubacher's perm and turned her flannel robe into a sodden mess. She didn't notice. "He knew when I wasn't happy, and never gave me any trouble. Since my Mack died, he's been my best friend. An old lady needs company."

Her every word fed my anger. Mrs. Frubacher had lived for her dog, and some asshole in a pickup truck had run over it for laughs. He might as well have run over Mrs. Frubacher and finished her then. I kept imagining that truck driver's nebulous face in the dirt whenever the shovel blade bit.

Five minutes later, I heaved the dog's body up out of the sweatshirt. Congealing blood smeared on my shirt. "It's ready."

Mrs. Frubacher moved up beside me. The rain accented the smell of her sachet. "Be happy, Sparky," she said, stroking the dangling muzzle and ears without noticing the blood. She was so wet that her whole body seemed covered with tears. "Be well."

A long moment later, she stepped back and bowed her head.

When I set the body in the grave, the sharp-edged shadows swallowed it instantly. I filled the hole as quickly as I could, Mrs. Frubacher watching silently.

Finally, I put the shovel away and threw my sweatshirt onto the garage trash can. Mrs. Frubacher followed me to the sidewalk. I turned to her and said "Good night." Not likely. "Try to sleep."

"Thank you, Mr. Keith."

I stumbled homeward, too exhausted to move and too furious to collapse. Rain dropped heavily around me.

By the time I got to my four-room house at the end of the street, mixed rage, fatigue, and cold made me quiver uncontrollably. I showered, but the hot water renewed the coppery stink. I kept finding flakes of dried dog's blood under my fingernails and in my arm hair. Even my waterbed's warm comfort didn't soothe me. The truck driver's laughter and the wet sound of a broken life bouncing on the sidewalk kept ricocheting in my ears. I couldn't get comfortable lying on my stomach or on my back or on my side.

The digital clock beside my bed had just changed to 3:08 AM when someone whispered "Matthew."

I sat up.

"Matthew." The whisper wasn't any louder.

"Who's there?" I pulled the sheet around me, for once regretting that I slept naked.

"Remember Haldeman." The voice sounded like wind whistling through the cracked window.

I jackknifed out of bed, pulled on a bathrobe, and walked into the living room. "Hello? Who's there?"

Silence.

I called out again. The voice didn't return. After my third fruitless circuit of the house, I swallowed a sleeping pill and dropped off.

The next morning, I didn't allow myself to think about Mrs. Frubacher or her dog. I treated myself to a long shower that didn't smell of blood, and to a five-egg mushroom-and-onion omelette. My muscle aches had faded to a dull burn. I dismissed the whispers as a dream.

I did the dishes and got to work at eleven, mostly clear-headed despite only five hours of sleep. The emergency room was quiet, except for an intermittent electronic beep and the squeals of a young girl having her broken leg set. Most of the staff stood in a cluster around the nurse's station, talking quietly. After last night's chaos, the sterile smells of bleach and disinfectant comforted me.

I walked up to the group, tugging my collar. The biggest hospital scrubs I've found are about two inches and twenty pounds too small. "Hi, what's up?"

Ted, another aide, said "Hi, Matt. It's Doctor Haldeman."

"What, he's reporting us all?"

Nurse O'Connor said, "He won't be reporting anyone. He's in ICU at Oakland General."

"What?"

An ambulance driver sipped his coffee. "The power steering on his Buick blew out down on I-696. He bounced off a brick wall at eighty miles an hour. They took him out with a can opener. He'll be lucky if he lives through the week."

I felt a sudden burst of vindication, which I forcefully quashed. A jerk deserves to lose his job, not his life.

The receiving doors jerked open as an aide rushed in, pushing a man in a wheelchair. We launched into motion.

I worked automatically, changing sheets and mopping blood with unthinking skill. Fortunately, the shift was physically easy: a couple of accidents, a man stabbed in a mugging, a woman who had "fallen down the stairs" during a visit from her boyfriend, and a few other examples of people hurting each other for no good reason.

I came home and collapsed in a chair. My arms and legs ached from the previous night, and my mind kept swirling. I was too tired to run. My anger had become a dull black lump in my gut. Had I really dreamt the voice? Was Haldeman's accident a coincidence? Even a heaping plate of spaghetti with heavily-spiced tomato sauce didn't soothe me.

After dinner I called my brother to chat for a few minutes, then got a beer and settled down to relax with a few old Hong Kong martial arts flicks. I had just started watching when the voice whispered, "'Dogs, driven wild...'"

I sat up straight. "Who's there?"

"'...break their chains, and escape from distant farms.'" I heard the soft words clearly over the blaring television.

I stood. "Come out here before I hurt you."

"'They run through the landscape, a prey to madness.' You ever feel that, Matthew? Prey to madness?"

My dinner became putty in my guts. Sweat slipped down my back. "This isn't funny," I said loudly, turning off the television.

The voice whispered "Call me Jeremiah. Lautreamont knew, you know. A brilliant man. And I smashed Haldeman to show my good faith."

"Where the hell are you?" I darted into the bathroom and flipped on the light. Nobody.

"Perhaps you mean 'what the hell are you?' I'm yours. I'm not your secret friend. I'm not even really a friend, just someone whom you're stuck with as I'm stuck with you. There's a lot to like about you, though. You're so likable that I like needing to like you."

I marched into the bedroom. "You're just pissing me off more."

"Try the closet. Maybe I'm in there."

I had already been moving towards the closet. The suggestion only made me angrier. I threw the door open and repeatedly jabbed my fist among the hanging clothes.

"You won't be happy until you search the refrigerator," Jeremiah said. "Go ahead."

The window looked like a huge black eye. I jerked the curtains shut. "What do you think you're doing?"

"I was in the dog. We're all in dogs, you know. Sometimes we can get out. Let's watch the news."

The television blared in the other room, and I jumped. I ran into the front room, closed both curtains, and sucked a deep breath. I thought that whoever was pulling this stunt must have had a remote control that worked on my television. My gaze darted through the room, looking for hidden speakers. Nothing. I leaned against the wall between the windows, checking the dusty corners.

The television changed to a local news show, and I started when I saw the truck stopped on the highway. I recognized the luggage rack and the large drums in the back. If the camera moved around to the front I'd probably recognize a dog-sized dent in its front bumper.

The tires were still burning. The rest of the truck had already scorched down to crusty metal. The announcer said that the wreck had blocked traffic for almost an hour. The driver had been burned alive.

"Merry Christmas," Jeremiah said.

I sat down heavily on the carpet.

The television went dead. "Now," Jeremiah said, "shall we talk?"

I shook my head.

"Don't be like that, Matthew." The kitchen and bedroom lights went out. "The lightning was close enough to start me, but the electricity in here is like the plumpest fruit. Kind of like kiwi. I've been stuck for such a long time."

My tongue finally worked. "Stuck where? Did you kill that driver?"

"You wanted him dead," Jeremiah said. "I was just saying thank you."

"You can't kill people, nothing's worth that."

"But you wanted him dead. Like you wanted Haldeman dead."

"I did not want them dead!"

"Yes, you did. And whenever you want someone dead, I'll take care of it for you."

"I don't want anyone dead," I said quickly. "Even a pustule like Haldeman doesn't deserve to die."

"You feel they do."

"You can't go around killing people, no matter how scummy they are. You — "

The ringing phone made me jump. Jeremiah said, "It's a telemarketer," as I snatched up the receiver.

"Hello?"

"Good evening sir," a voice said with false cheer, "I'm with Home Service — "

"Go away." I slammed the phone down, breathing heavily.

"You learn to do lots of stuff when you're stuck in a dog's head. I still can't do chess problems, though."

"They've been trying to sell me maid service for six months. Easy guess."

Jeremiah said something. I stopped listening. Most of the patients in the hospital's psychiatric wing got there by hearing voices or slashing their wrists. If he didn't shut up, I'd have to check myself in.

The whispers grew more insistent.

I started singing nursery rhymes.

The ringing doorbell shattered my concentration. Jeremiah fell silent as I leaped to my feet.

Mrs. Frubacher jumped in surprise when I flung the door open. The wrinkles on her face were black crevasses under the porch light. She wore a pink fake fur coat and had covered her hair with a scarf. Her right hand fluttered towards her mouth, her left held a plastic bag. Behind her, the wind slowly gyrated the bare branches of the trees along the street.

I took a deep breath and arranged a smile on my face. "Hello, Mrs. Frubacher. What can I do for you?"

"I… hello, Mr. Keith." Her voice trembled slightly. "You left your sweatshirt in my garage. I washed it for you."

"Thanks."

She smiled again, and a hint of red colored her cheeks. "Mr. Keith, I'd like to ask you a favor. Would you take me to the Humane Society tomorrow?"

"We don't need her, Matthew," Jeremiah whispered. "Get rid of her."

I jerked to look behind me. Mrs. Frubacher said "Do you have company?"

I turned back to her just as quickly. "No. No, why?"

"I thought I heard someone."

"It's just me. You said something about the Humane Society?"

"I hate to ask, but the minibus people won't let me take a dog with me."

"You're getting another dog?"

She nodded.

"Sure. I'd be glad to help." I didn't want to get up that early, but Jeremiah wanted me to get rid of her. "I have to be at work at eleven, but could I take you at, say, eight?"

Her blush spread towards her eyes and mouth. "That would be wonderful."

"I'll see you then."

Mrs. Frubacher turned away. I closed and locked the door.

She'd heard the voice.

Every room except the living room was dark. I sat down in my chair. "Jeremiah?"

Nothing answered.

I searched the apartment twice, calling out all the time, but nobody answered. Finally I put on a clean sweatsuit and went to bed. I dreamed of lightning and blood.

The dogs hated us.

Mrs. Frubacher and I stood in a narrow aisle between wire pens. I'd never seen more dogs in one place. The larger ones clawed at the fences, growling and barking and stepping in their dishes in their frenzy to reach us. The chorus echoed around the close brick walls, deafening both of us. I saw a mutt as large as me biting the wire fence, the white around its eyes bloodshot as it tried to attack us. Smaller dogs hugged the brick walls, watching us and snarling.

Mrs. Frubacher stood straight, clutching her purse in both hands. Her face sagged with disappointment. "They don't seem to have any nice ones."

"We could try another place some other morning."

She nodded primly, and we turned to go.

I thought I heard whispers behind me. I didn't look.

As I closed the door to the kennels behind us, the dogs fell silent. The girl working behind the lobby desk looked at us curiously. "Is everything all right?"

"Fine, thank you, miss," Mrs. Frubacher said stiffly as we started for the outside door.

The day was chilly and clear, with only a few clouds in an achingly blue sky. As I pulled my crackerbox car into traffic, Mrs. Frubacher said "Thank you for driving."

"You're welcome." I didn't like the way she rigidly watched the car's hood. "The city pound has dogs, too."

"I'm afraid that won't do, Mr. Keith. I've never seen dogs as vicious as those — especially at the Humane Society. I simply can't imagine how bad they are at the pound."

Dropping her off at home, I headed for work. I thought she'd find a bridge club, or take up shuffleboard, or whatever else it was that old people did. When I merged into the crowded highway, Jeremiah whispered "Stupid old woman."

I didn't even twitch. "She's a nice lady."

"Yes, she is. 'Come here, Sparky. Have some cake, Sparky. You're a saint, Sparky.' The damn dog liked it, too. Sickening. I can't wait for her to put her head in that gas oven. Do you play chess?"

"That dog was her world! Why don't you just go away?"

"I can't. I'll be White; King's Knight to King's Bishop 3."

"What do you want, anyway?"

"'For a long time now the moonbeams have been shining on the marble tombstones.' Ever read Lautreamont?"

"What do you want?" I changed lanes, squeezing my rattling compact between a decrepit Buick sedan and a Lincoln Town Car.

"Too bad. You should. I hope he's still in print."

"Go. Away."

"I can't. You let me out. I'm stuck with you. Do you like Brahms?"

"Then what *are* you?"

"I can't stand him, either. I'm like you, like a fish, like a tree. We've always been here, since your great-great grandpa domesticated a wolf. Your feelings chose me. If you'd been happy when the mutt got smeared, you'd've gotten someone different. There's a cop around the next bend."

"How can I get rid of you?" My hands felt clammy on the vinyl steering wheel, and I hit the brake more forcefully than I should have. The Town Car behind me blasted its horn and flashed its headlights. It backed off when the cop came into view.

"Not telling. Can I route all of that telemarketer's calls to Albuquerque?"

"You can do that?"

"Consider it done. Checkers?"

"I don't play games."

"Your move."

He wouldn't say anything else until I got home that night.

This conversation recurred in various forms over the next month. He wouldn't tell me what he was, he wouldn't be serious, but he would help me.

At work, Jeremiah told me what to have ready. Before someone threw up, I had a clean mop on hand. When a horribly burned patient came in, I "happened" to have the burn equipment out. I had crash carts ready before any patient's heart stopped. Over the next month, ER casualties dropped twenty percent.

It surprises me that my routine absorbed Jeremiah so easily. Not only did telemarketers stop bothering me, but whenever the phone rang Jeremiah told me who was calling. The last person who cut me off on the highway had car trouble half a mile later. I stopped collecting traffic tickets.

I got the Lautreamont book from the library. After reading a few pages I flipped through the rest, and threw it down. Every page described atrocities, and incomprehensible atrocities at that. I considered seeing a priest, but didn't bother. If God wouldn't help a fifteen-year-old girl tied up in the back of a van, he sure wouldn't help me. Sometimes when Jeremiah spoke I looked around closely, hoping to see anything that might betray his presence. I never saw any hint of him.

Dogs hated me, though. When I went running, a stream of panicked and infuriated barks erupted from half the houses I passed. I occasionally thought I heard incomprehensible whispers in the barks. After a Pekingese leapt out of its owner's arms to try to bite my face, I started crossing the street to avoid people with dogs. A neighbor's German Shepherd broke its chain and chased me half a mile, and I began carrying pepper spray.

I didn't tell anyone about Jeremiah. I had a gut feeling that he'd remain silent precisely when I bet my apparent sanity on him. I couldn't even tell my brother Eric, even though we spent a couple hours a week talking about everything else. When I visited Eric and Donna for three days at Christmas, I didn't mention Jeremiah and Jeremiah didn't do anything. In January, I returned for my niece Samantha's fourth birthday.

I settled by the grand piano, just behind the circle of relatives, to watch her open her presents. I'd brought a stuffed bear slightly smaller than she was and a set of Dr. Seuss books for Eric to read to her. Her favorite gift seemed to be a miniature xylophone from my Aunt Beth. Eric's upward glance told me that that particular toy would quickly find a home in the dustiest corner of the basement.

After Samantha had opened her last present, Eric told her to wait for a moment. She squeezed her eyes closed. Eric vanished upstairs. He returned moments later and set a white terrier puppy in her lap.

She opened her eyes and squealed with delight. Jeremiah unexpectedly whispered "Oooh" in my ear. I smiled and clapped like everyone else, but my guts suddenly felt an electric tingle. The puppy seemed a younger version of Mrs. Frubacher's Sparky.

"I'll call him Ralph," Samantha said.

The dog stopped squirming, looked towards me, and stared like it recognized something. It wasn't me.

Half an hour later, I told Eric that I wasn't feeling well and I should go home. He frowned and walked me to the door. "Is it something you ate?" he asked. "Donna didn't put meat in the lasagna."

I shook my head. "I just feel odd. I might be coming down with a bug."

"Then stay here tonight."

I stayed more often than not, but I shook my head. "Tomorrow's Superbowl Sunday, the biggest day of the year for battered women in ER."

"Yeah, you've told me." Eric frowned. "Listen, Matt, I keep getting a feeling something's wrong. Is there something you haven't told me?"

I have a murderous invisible companion who likes dead French poets and your kid's dog. "No, I can't think of anything."

"You've always got a place here, you know."

I tried to smile. "Thanks. I'll give you a call next week."

I'd hardly put the car into gear and waved goodbye when Jeremiah whispered "Can I have a puppy? How about that one?"

"That's my niece's! And I won't have a dog in the house."

"Oh, I won't bring it home. You'll have to do the work, though. Where should we kill it?"

"You can't do *anything* to Sam's dog! Do you understand? Nothing!"

Jeremiah just started reciting weird stuff about moons and blood and some sleeping hermaphrodite. He could rattle on for hours, and I quickly turned on the radio to drown him out. Out in this countryside, I could only find the farm report and a station commemorating its shift to classic rock by cycling through all forty-seven covers of "Louie, Louie." The song made more sense than Jeremiah's ranting.

My hands clenched the steering wheel more tightly than usual. I didn't know how many lives I'd saved since Jeremiah started giving me advance warning. I'd always considered myself a fighter against Death — not an officer, but at least a sturdy foot soldier. Now I was moving up through the ranks. Would I have to kill my niece's dog to save lives?

In the garage, I turned off the car. Jeremiah's voice was suddenly loud in the silence. "' — riddled with lice. Hugs, when they look at me, vomit. My skin is encrusted — '"

"You don't have skin, and I'm not listening."

I loudly hummed as I watched the sun go down. Jeremiah never took a breath. His inflectionless voice never showed strain as he recited atrocities and impossibilities and simple descriptions of flying birds. He ignored my demands for quiet.

About eight that night, I stuffed cotton in my ears. The earplugs squeezed all the color from Jeremiah's voice, but I still heard him. Clapping my hands over my ears reduced his voice to an unintelligible murmur. I tried to focus my thoughts on the newspaper, but I found myself unwillingly straining for his muffled words instead.

I tried a pair of full-size headphones. I hardly slipped them on when his words became crystal-clear. Obviously, if Jeremiah could change television channels, he could send his voice over speakers. I wrenched the headphones off and threw them against the wall, cracking the plaster.

I turned the radio on.

He turned it off without missing a syllable.

"Shut up!" I shouted, my throat raw from hours of humming.

"' — skin of his brow has been so stretched by his hanging that his face — '"

"Leave me alone!"

I broke out in a sweat. Sometime in the last few minutes, my hands had begun trembling. I kept trying to hum, then read aloud, but my throat was too raw. If I hadn't already known that Jeremiah didn't have a body, I would have torn the place apart to strangle him.

About ten that night, I took a shower to try to relax. To my surprise, the white noise of running water drowned Jeremiah's voice. After a fast run I slept on the bathroom floor, repeatedly bumping my head on the toilet bowl. The shower's gurgle and splash formed unintelligible words, but they weren't Jeremiah's.

I awoke the next morning with a stiff neck and an irresistible urge to urinate. Dim light leaked through the bathroom window's frosted glass. I smelled mildew. The shower's gurgle seemed a normal part of the world. When I shut off the water, the silence made me smile. Jeremiah had given up.

I walked into my living room.

The television exploded.

Glass showered out of the socket where the picture tube had been, and I smelled burning insulation. I dashed across the room and jerked the plug out of the wall. The plastic felt warm in my hand, and I thought it twitched weakly, like a dying creature's pulse.

Jeremiah whispered, "Oops."

I tensed my jaw, and forcibly relaxed. Glass crackled under my feet as I pulled on my clothes and left for work an hour early.

ER was equally quiet when I arrived. I was leaning against a gurney sipping my second coffee when Nurse Anderson shouted "Crash cart!"

I spilled the coffee down the front of my scrubs. Before Jeremiah, that shout wouldn't have made me even flinch. Last week, I would have been standing there with the cart. I was running in a heartbeat, though, and had the cart in the doctor's hands in fifteen seconds. Minutes later, another call surprised me.

Jeremiah would make me beg for his help. It wouldn't stop with one dog, however. I'd wind up in prison as a mad dog killer.

I worked hard enough. Nobody died.

I left the hospital more exhausted than I had been since Jeremiah's appearance, with a few stubborn bits of puke knotting my hair. I folded myself into my car, dreaming of a hot shower and clean clothes.

At the corner of Eleven Mile and Main, half a mile from home, I glided into a green light only to hear a barrage of horns. I glanced around and saw two cars braking hard, horns blaring.

I stomped on the accelerator, and my car lurched out of the way with a three-cylinder sputter. My face was sweating, and I shivered. Jeremiah had made the traffic lights all turn green.

Everything at home was as I had left it. Cleaning up the wrecked television would take hours, and I'd catch occasional splinters of glass in my feet for months. Damn him.

I marched to the refrigerator for a beer, planning to relax for two minutes before attacking the mess. The handle felt warm, but I didn't think anything of that. As I swung the door open, however, an wave of hot moist odor spilled out. The leftovers had blown off their plastic lids. The beer cans had boiled and burst.

I slammed the door and marched to the counter. With one sweep I unplugged the blender and the can opener, then I jerked the clock plug out of the wall. The plug for the living room stereo was buried behind the stereo rack, but two hard swipes with a broom tore it out. Darkness flooded the living room and kitchen when I pulled the lamp plugs. I unplugged the waterbed heater and the bedroom clock, then advanced to the basement and jerked all the circuit breakers out of the box.

"It won't help, Matthew," Jeremiah said. "Your neighbors have plenty of power for me. Why don't you just kill the dog? I'll teach you to play chess."

"Go to hell."

"I thought we passed this stage in our relationship. You really ought to read Lautreamont. You'd understand so much better."

"It's unreadable, and I'm not doing a damned thing to Samantha's dog."

"It's not a damned thing. It's a good thing."

"I'm don't care."

"It's part of me in there," Jeremiah said. "Do you think that all of me could fit inside one dog? There's bits and pieces of me scattered in a hundred different dogs, crammed in with other pieces of others just like me. Your niece has one of those pieces. I need your passion to free me. Heal me, and I'll be of greater help to you."

I looked around my basement, at the dead electric dryer and the silent freezer. "I don't want anything from you."

"Do you know why I helped you at work? To make you happy. The next time you run for a defibrillator I think I'll suck the power out of it. Everyone who annoys you will die, Matthew. Tailgaters. Doctors. Little kids laughing loudly. And you'll know it's your fault. Learn to like it. At least you haven't known any of the people who've died so far."

"What?"

"You called me in anger, Matthew. You chose who I was."

"Who else? What have you *done*?"

"It's amazing how much I can do with a little spark."

A noise too loud to be heard filled the air, gently pressing from all directions. The house seemed to lift up a fraction of an inch, and I felt my feet leave the floor.

My weight returned.

"Say, a gas explosion," Jeremiah said, his voice flat after that shocking roar, "when an old lady has her head in the oven."

I ran upstairs and dashed outside, ignoring the cold January wind. Bits of wood and fragments of brick rained on the street and in the snowbanks. The streetlights battled the flickering light from the burning shell that had been Mrs. Frubacher's house, casting red and yellow reflections across the crusty snow. I smelled charcoal and gas. "Jeremiah! Jeremiah, you bastard!"

"Oh, she was doing herself in anyway," he whispered. "She hasn't been taking care of herself since her dog died, just moping around that house without seeing anyone. She really was too dependent on that mutt, you know. I told you so, you'll recall."

A police car turned onto the street and I realized how I looked, standing in the middle of the street without a coat and screaming. I trotted back into the house and slammed the door.

"Jeremiah, you're — "

" — A sick puppy? Can't you be original?"

I closed my eyes and took a deep breath, trying to control the tremors that raced up and down my body. I wanted to return to the night old lady Frubacher's dog died and kick the mutt's body back into the street. Instead, I opened my eyes and said "I'm going to call my brother."

"Tell him to bring the dog."

"It's none of your business what I tell him." I picked up the handset. The line was dead. "Stop fucking with the phone, asshole."

The dial tone returned, and I punched Eric's number. As the first ring echoed, I realized that my brother would be asleep by now. The phone rang four times before Donna sleepily said "Hello?"

"Hi, Donna, it's Matt. I know it's late, but I need to talk to Eric." Sirens in the background added their urgency to my voice. I could smell smoke again.

She mumbled grumpily, then I heard a rustle. After several heartbeats, Eric said "Hello?" He sounded more alert than I expected.

"Eric, I've got a problem, I need your help."

"Name it."

"Can you take tomorrow off and come down here?"

"Sure. What's up?"

"I'd rather tell you in person."

He paused. "All right."

"Oh, and Eric, come alone."

"What?"

"Come alone. I don't want this to go any farther than it has to."

After a long pause, Eric said "All right, no problem."

"I'll be here all day. I'm calling in sick. Get here as soon as you can."

"Will do. Are you going to be all right tonight?"

He was awake wondering about me, I realized. I felt ashamed for not telling him before. "I'll be fine. I think I'll sleep well tonight."

"Good. Be careful."

"I will. Thanks, Eric."

"Any time."

I said goodbye and hung up, then snarled and kicked the wall as hard as I could. "You better not touch anyone tonight, bastard," I shouted. "You so much as twitch, and I'll get him to take that dog somewhere you'll never find it. Do you understand me?"

Jeremiah said nothing.

"Do you?" I kicked the wall again. It didn't help. Finally, I replaced the circuit breakers and went out for veggie tacos and a long, long run.

⚜

The next morning I called in sick. I considered cleaning my house, but decided against it. The smell of boiled refrigerator and the glitter of glass in the carpet would make an impression on Eric. I just hoped that I wanted to make that particular impression. I made coffee and stood by the front window to watch work crews clean the street. Both the gas and electric companies had trucks out. City workers shoveled bits of Mrs. Frubacher's house, and probably bits of Mrs. Frubacher, into a shiny dump truck. Last night's fire had coated the snow in my front yard with a thick crust of ice.

Eric drove up to the curb just after eleven, parking right behind the electric company's cherry-picker working at a power pole. I set the coffee cup down and wiped my forehead. "Jeremiah," I said, "will you show yourself?"

Silence.

Eric climbed out of the truck. A second later, the passenger door opened and Samantha climbed out, wearing a heavy coat and carrying her puppy in her arms.

I bolted outside. "Eric! I told you to come alone!"

He frowned. "No, you told me to bring Sam and her dog. Are you all right?"

I abruptly felt the bite of frozen concrete through my socks, and realized that I'd once again dashed out into the sub-zero wind without shoes or a coat. "No, I don't think so." Jeremiah meant to have that dog. "Could Sam and the dog play in the yard for a few minutes while we talk?"

Samantha's face quivered, and she held the puppy tightly. The dog stopped squirming to watch me. I said, "It's all right, Samantha. I just need to talk to your dad."

Eric's eyes never left my face. "You and Ralph play outside for a little while, Samantha."

I ushered Eric in and waved to Samantha. She stared at me with scared blue eyes, as if she thought I'd flipped. Maybe I had.

Eric looked shocked when he came in, and his nose wrinkled at the smell. "What's up, Matt?"

I closed the front door and shook my head. "I'm not sure. Do you want coffee?"

"No, I'd like to know what's going on."

"Watch out for glass in the carpet."

"I am. What's going on, Matt?"

I sat down heavily on my chair. "His name is Jeremiah, and he wants me to kill Samantha's dog, and I'm sure he changed my words on the phone last night so you heard me tell you to bring him up. He can play with electricity, somehow."

Eric slipped out of his coat, watching me carefully. His feet crunched in broken glass as he dragged the kitchen chair over to face me and sat down. "Who is he? We'll get the police on him!"

"That'd be great, if anyone could see him."

Eric's eyes narrowed. "He's invisible?"

"I don't think he's even really there. Do you believe in ghosts?"

"You think you're haunted?"

"That's as good as anything. He's been doing little stuff for me until now, but he thinks that part of him is stuck in Sam's dog. He wants me to kill the mutt to let it out." I waved my hands around at the ruins of my apartment. "He blew up the TV, he made the refrigerator boil, he mucked with traffic lights and killed God knows how many people..."

Eric had grown almost rigid. He watched me very carefully.

"If I don't kill the dog, he'll ruin my life. If I do, he'll get more powerful."

Eric nodded slowly. "That's a problem."

I said "Do you think I don't know how this sounds? He talks to me when nobody else is around. I'm hearing a voice."

"Have you seen a doctor?"

Ralph started barking. I sat up straight. His yaps had the same frenzy that the dogs in the pound and on the street had had around me. "He's outside! Samantha!" I shouted. Eric was only inches behind me as I launched myself at the front door.

Samantha stood hip-deep in the icy snow in front of the house, holding the straining puppy's leash. The dog, almost invisible against the snow, sat down and wagged its tail, then jerked onto its rear feet and started barking at the electric company's cherry-picker again as the workmen worked at the pole. Abruptly, the twenty-foot-tall hydraulic arm was swinging away from the pole, over the street. The man in the basket shouted "Jake!" as he grabbed at the controls. "Cut the power, Jake!"

Ralph rolled over, splaying his feet in the air. Playing dead.

Samantha was looking at Ralph, shaking her head. "What's wrong, boy?" He convulsed to his feet and barked again.

The worker in the truck cab did something I couldn't see, then shouted, "It won't shut off!"

"Samantha, come here," called Eric. His left hand held my shoulder firmly. "Matt, come on in, it's okay. We'll take care of it."

The cherry-picker box was perpendicular to the power line in front of my house. The hydraulic motor suddenly hummed loudly, and the entire arm swung towards us. The worker in the basket shouted as the box crashed against the power line, forcing it towards my house and over Sam.

I leapt off the porch and dashed towards her, my bare feet crashing through the ice into knee-deep snow with every step. "Get back, Sam!"

The lines held, and the arm pulled back for another swing.

Ralph wagged his tail, then snapped at me. The piece of Jeremiah in it was happy. He'd said that dogs held parts of other creatures like him. Those other parts, some of the other parts, weren't happy. The dog's body ricocheted between Jeremiah and them.

Eric shouted something.

Samantha turned towards me, her face widening in fear. She was only a few feet away when one of my feet didn't go through the crust of ice, skidding instead.

I windmilled one arm and threw the other foot forward, my free hand reaching out for Samantha.

I couldn't stay upright. I was going to fall.

My hand clenched Samantha's jacket.

The worker overhead shouted, "Get away from there!" The power line overhead crackled as it snapped.

I wrenched at Sam's coat and threw her towards Eric. She let go of the leash and skidded across the ice. The throw destroyed what little balance I had.

Both my feet flew into the air. I landed on my back, crashing through the ice into the snow. Something smashed into the back of my head, then a loud thrumming swallowed my mind. The impact emptied my lungs.

I tried to suck a breath.

I couldn't.

Ralph barked at me, then sunk its teeth into my left calf. I would have shouted, if I could have breathed.

Snow blocked my view in every direction except overhead. The sparking power line twitched towards me, as if someone guided it.

"The stupid worker almost killed Sam," Jeremiah whispered. "Hate him for it. Call me out of the dog, I'll hurt him for you."

All I could think was *Jeremiah, you bastard* as I struggled to breathe.

The power line touched.

Then my legs thrashed and my back arched against my will. I couldn't feel my body. My jaw locked closed. I heard nothing except Jeremiah's bubbly laughter. I stopped trying to breathe. I wanted to rip Jeremiah apart. The smell of roast meat filled my head.

Hate fed Jeremiah. He was growing. I'd be stuck with him forever. He'd kill hundreds.

The thought revolted me. Jeremiah revolted me.

Then Jeremiah shouted "No!" He screamed like a tea kettle, then his cry shattered into different tones and faded.

The next convulsion beat my head against the ground and threw me aside.

An unfamiliar voice whispered "It is done. Goodbye."

Then I didn't think of anything at all.

I heard Eric's voice before I awoke. I couldn't understand his words, but they kept me warm in the same way that the familiar sour hospital smell comforted me. I was at work, where I belonged, doing what I was meant to do. Even if I couldn't tell what that was. For a while, I heard Donna's voice as well.

When I finally awoke enough to assemble my senses, I saw Eric beside my hospital bed. He leaned closer, frowning. "How are you doing?"

I'm in the hospital. My head hurts, and I probably have electrical burns over half my body. "Okay." *My throat hurts, too.*

He smiled. "Good. Samantha's all right."

I nodded. The motion made me notice my bandaged head and the dull pulsing in the back of my skull.

"The doctor says you'll be fine," Eric continued. "You've got a nasty lump on the back of your head, a chunk out of your leg, a couple burns, but your heart's all right. You're lucky the power line touched Ralph and not you."

After he mentioned it, I could feel pain in my leg. "Thanks." There was a dusty spot on the wall. I would've cleaned a room better than this before moving a patient in.

Eric sat silently for a long moment, and I closed my eyes. The darkness seemed to dampen the pain in my head.

Finally Eric asked "What was that?"

"What was what?"

"That voice. That *scream*. I've never heard anything like it."

"That was Jeremiah. I think he's dead."

"Oh."

"The first time, I was mad at people and got Jeremiah. This time, I hated Jeremiah in particular. I called something that hated him, killed him." I closed my eyes.

Eric sat silently for a few moments, then made me promise to visit soon. I think we both need a night of that peculiar honest conversation only possible when moderately drunk.

Shortly after Eric left, Doctor Haldeman walked through the hall. He had an arm in a sling and stitches across his face, but he still made everyone jump out of his way. If Jeremiah needed to kill, why hadn't Haldeman died and Mrs. Frubacher lived?

Doctor Ellers wants to keep me overnight. I'd like to go home tomorrow, but I don't know if I can.

I've been lying here in bed watching television and remembering why I don't watch the news. Wars on three continents. Robbery. Rape. Murder. People keep aiming and accelerating until they run over each other. A few months ago, my helplessness against it all would have made me furious.

Now, I just feel cold.

I don't know what they are, or why I can call them. I do know that emotions define them and electricity gives them life. The biggest power plant in the world is up in Quebec, only about fifteen hours away. I'm sure I could find dogs up there.

They're not subtle. Maybe that's because I'm not. It would be a brutal peace. But I don't know if it could be worse than what we have now.

All I've ever wanted to scream to the world is, "Be nice to each other."

OPENING THE EYE

I found the drill in a maggoty dumpster.

Burns pocked its plastic case, and the two-inch circular doorknob bit clenched in its maw was rusty and dull. Bare wire frayed through the layer of electrical tape wrapped around its cord; I replaced it with one from a toaster oven hoping the secondhand shop around the corner would give me five bucks for it. And five bucks equaled one hit. Five bucks erected that sweet, unbreakable barrier between me and the world where I could watch and touch, but not be touched.

I wanted to spend that five bucks bad, but there was a drought in the city — no crack, no speed, no oblivion.

I knew what I had to do.

Two of my five bucks bought a new drill bit. The hardware store was out of one-eights, so I took a three-sixteenth. The bit's length worried me more than the width; if it was too short, it wouldn't puncture bone. I left the bit in the shrink-wrap, to keep it clean.

I could do this.

The syringe was new, too, its contents guaranteed to make me numb. It had cost me my last three bucks and a favor I was working hard to forget.

It had to work.

Before the cable got cut off, I'd watched Joey Mellen drill an eighth-inch hole in his head, right over his pineal gland; he claimed that the rest of his life would be one long natural high. The TV commentator called it "trepanation."

Trepanation. I liked the sound of that word. I didn't know what the pineal gland was, but the TV people showed me where to find it: right under the skull in the center of my forehead.

For cheap excitement, I could go outside and get myself beat up again, but it wasn't enough.

I needed more.

The drill's two-inch wide doorknob bit watched me with tetanus eyes.

Unless something happened soon, I'd start gnawing my fingers, focused on the thought of a single hit to soften the clawing hunger in my bones, and hating myself because I couldn't stop. Even if I wanted to.

It might not work. The drill might not get through the bone. Or I might cut too deep. And I wasn't *really* trapped; climb through the window to the new high of the fifth floor and open air and a concrete sidewalk below.

I snatched up the drill and wrenched out the filthy bit. Its plastic shroud tore easily, and I cranked the drill chuck around it tight.

Sitting crosslegged on the floor before the cracked mirror, I cradled the drill in my lap and picked up the needle. The mirror distorted my image, showing skin hung loose from bone, long beard irreparably tangled. Only two years ago I'd been so proud of that beard, but that's life when you're smoking the devil's prick. My heart beat so hard it made the syringe quiver in my fingers. At first the needle bowed faintly against my skull, making me hold my breath, but finally the tip slid against the bone and I eased the plunger down. Tingling iciness trickled out from the needle, weighting my eyebrows and making my forehead move some place far away. My breath came fast and hard as my heartbeat became a ponderous thump in wrists and ankles.

I pulled the needle out and probed my forehead, feeling leaden numbness ripple out from my eyebrows up the scalp under my widow's peak and towards my temples. After a few minutes, when it seemed that the freeze had traveled far enough, I gripped the drill in both hands, my fingers reversed around the grip and my thumbs overlapping on the trigger.

Mirrors always confuse me. Every time I'd try to knot a necktie or pop a zit, my movements would end up backwards. Now, I turned the drill one way and it went another. It took awhile to get the bit pointing straight at my forehead, arms raised over my head so I could see in the reflection where the tip dimpled my skin.

I pushed the trigger with both thumbs. The noise shocked me, arriving at my brain without passing through my ears, a grinding rattle in my skull that made a dentist's drill sound like elevator music. My teeth clanged together, and the scent of burning meat filled my nostrils.

The fog of fine-spraying blood around the hole made it difficult to see my reflection, but I glimpsed thin shreds of skin whirling away from the screaming bit. I clenched the drill closer, and the motor's roar deepened as it met new resistance. A curl of white bone nudged out of the hole.

The noise grew even louder.

My nerves came back to life, but there was no pain. Instead, strangely, the drill bit conjured up the most incredible taste I'd ever experienced, like garlic cooked for days until the sharpness disappears and only an intense flavor remains. Thoughts of my last roommate's spaghetti sauce flitted through my mind. The drill bucked in my hands.

The drill had skewed. I let the motor slow and pushed it back to straighten the bit, letting it spin freely. The air smelled of copper and heated metal and flesh; the hot motor stung my hands.

I pushed the trigger down again, hard, and *pulled*.

Noise swallowed my thoughts.

The drill sunk half an inch and spun free. I released the trigger and pushed the motor back. Blood scattered like cake batter from mixer blades.

My reflection stared back at me. The new eye gleamed red and black. I'd never seen a look so shocked and relieved on anyone's face before.

My forehead throbbed.

I think I dropped the drill. My muscles relaxed simultaneously, and I fell backwards against the couch and onto the floor.

My forehead pulsed again. The throb wasn't from my skin, but somewhere deeper. My eyes wouldn't focus or close. The throb, warm and peaceful, washed through my head and into my neck. The naked light bulb dangling from the ceiling burned the corner of my vision, but I couldn't turn away.

Throb. Womblike warmth hit my spine. I smiled.

Throb. My hands grew light. Each knuckle tingled separately.

Throb. The soles of my feet burned, unbearably alive in their cramped shoes.

I still couldn't blink.

One more throb, and I was whole. I felt like a sunny day, like sex and steak, whiskey and winning. The addiction I'd etched into my bones over the last few years was still there, and just as insistent, but it didn't matter anymore.

Peace.

My stomach growled, and I finally blinked. When had I last eaten? Yesterday? The day before? I felt like I could consume a Cadillac.

Eventually, I lifted my head. The world swirled around me. Crack had made the world as untouchable as I was, and the unexpected intimacy of my apartment stunned me. The abrupt closeness of everything stunned me.

I'd always thought of my studio apartment as a real dump, had never noticed the delicate spiderweb of cracks in the windowpane, or the echoing circles in the water-stained ceiling. The interplay between the scents of gore and mildew astounded me. A flash of reflected light from the bent TV antenna was a hypnotic kaleidoscope. It could've held my attention forever, if I hadn't been so hungry.

I slowly sat back up, my head sloshing like a half-full glass of water.

The mirror told me that the bleeding seemed to have stopped.

I blinked again. A tangle of feathers hung from my new eye.

As I watched, the feathers twitched. I felt a slippery, sliding motion under my skull, as if someone had pulled the cloth off the table of my mind without disturbing the place settings. The feathers brushed gently against my forehead, then bloodlessly levered themselves free.

Not a bundle of feathers, not quite. More like a spider with countless feathery limbs curled in every direction. The feather-spider perched on my forehead for a moment, then drifted lightly to the floor.

It trotted one way, then another, like a beagle casting about for a scent. I smiled. I'd owned a beagle years ago. What had happened to her?

My eyes followed the feather-spider, then lost themselves in the kitchen alcove: food.

Holding my head level to minimize the sloshing, I clambered to my feet. Every time I lifted a foot, the ground moved and I had to find it again. Intricate stains and spatters mottled the kitchen cupboard's laminated surface. I stared at its scarred handle for a long moment, tracing thirty years of marks, before reaching out.

I felt every scratch on the handle.

Baked beans, cold and eaten with fingers straight from the can, had never tasted so rich, so full of salt and vegetable bite. I ate slowly, savoring each mouthful, letting the smeared sauce on my fingers send threads of pleasure up my arm. The throb in my head connected me to every chew and swallow, filling me with quiet joy until my hands were licked clean.

I stared at the empty can, watching the juice trickle sensuously down the label. How had I been so *blind*?

Back on the couch, each broken spring marking its own impression on my back and butt, my eyes roamed the ceiling as I traced the intricate pattern of cracks and stains, marveling at their complexity.

An hour or a minute later, my dream was broken by an ugly brittle scrape. The feather-spider crawled up the bent television antenna. With every inch it traveled, the antenna straightened out. Each brush of a feather-foot sucked away the chrome's luster.

The creature perched atop the repaired antenna for a second, then leapt down.

The antenna didn't interest me anymore.

The pattern of scars and burns on the wooden floor held my attention only until the feather-spider weaved drunkenly across the room and into my field of vision. The marks on the floor disappeared where it had passed, leaving only clean, dull wood. The creature started up the wall beside me, erasing the interesting array of bumps and nicks as it went. Then it scuttled to the window, healing the glass beneath it.

I shook my head, the throb washing from one ear to the other. My eyes wandered from the feather-spider to the David Byrne tour poster hanging beside the window, losing themselves in the interconnected wrinkles.

The rapture remained until the poster-paper rustled. The feather-spider sat on its edge, two raised front limbs caressing each other. The window was intact, but dull, the glass somehow sucking the flavor from the sunlight.

The feather-spider set out across the poster, leaving a plain white trail in its wake.

I took a pot from the kitchen sink and stared at the overlapping grains of decayed oatmeal. Then I took the lid in my other hand and walked towards the feather-spider. The floor beneath me shifted like the deck of a trawler on the open ocean.

By the time I reached the poster, the feather-spider had almost erased the entire top half. I lifted the pot and gingerly caged the creature against the wall.

The inside of the pot was probably becoming boringly clean. I flipped the pot gently, catching the feather-spider. Although it didn't have eyes, it watched me, interrupting my focus, stealing my pleasure.

I carried the pot back to the sink and picked up a big wooden spoon. Three sharp whacks, then a dozen more, each impact sending tickling vibrations through my hand. The feather-spider bounced back after each blow.

A splash of lighter fluid and a lit match made a puff of blue flame. The feather-spider raised a single unblackened limb over the edge of the pot and waved at me.

Grinding it with half a brick didn't work, either.

I pitched the spider out the window, five floors above the sidewalk.

Just as I settled into staring at the patterns woven into the faded couch, I glimpsed motion on the windowsill. The feather-spider dropped to the floor and started erasing scars.

Again, I scooped the creature up in the pot and replaced the lid, holding it down with my elbow. A feathery limb slid out between lid and pot. In another throb, the feather-spider sat beside me.

It looked at me.

Back in the pot it went.

I sat before the mirror, hands wrapped around the edge between pot and lid. The waves of quiet pleasure washing my mind couldn't obliterate sharp shards of concern. I had to do something with the feather-spider before it dulled my whole world.

My reflection stared back at me through the bloody mirror. The edges of my third eye were rough and black.

Inspiration made me smile.

The feather-spider needed to go back where it came from, but no way I could muscle it through that tiny red-black hole.

Decisions, decisions.

I picked up the drill and switched back to the two-inch doorknob bit.

"I told you a five-eights! This is a five-sixteenths!"

Father wouldn't have been mad, if she'd just done it right. Chris rummaged through the big toolbox. The greasy wrenches and screwdrivers were all churned together, and escaped her touch. She finally caught a larger wrench and handed it to Father.

Chris and her father were taking off the old basement door. She had almost clawed through it last time. The new door stood at an angle against the kitchen sink. Chris was sixteen years old. Hair was starting to grow on her face.

Of the many times Chris had been locked in the basement, she remembered the first time the best. Her twelfth birthday had hit only days before, and Father had actually laughed and sung and got her a junkyard bicycle he'd repaired and repainted. He'd hugged her, too. Mom had patted Chris on the head and told her "Happy Birthday."

That had been the last time anyone had touched her. It was also the last time that Father had been kind to her.

Chris was sweeping the bathroom's dusty tile after dinner when she noticed the hair on her hands. It was white and soft, like the first shoots of spring grass. Her hands had always been hairless; they'd been smooth an hour before. Her stomach squirmed around the peanut butter sandwich she'd had for dinner. She suddenly itched, everywhere.

The cracked bathroom mirror diagonally split her reflection. Short albino hair had appeared across her forehead and under her chin. She quivered, and hair sprouted below her eyes and spread across her cheeks.

Mom had come in then, probably to tell Chris to turn off the light and stop staring in the mirror. Mom's face was even thinner than Chris', and just as pale. Her eyes grew wide when she saw Chris caressing her furry face, then she turned and dashed through the hall towards the living room.

Chris turned back to the mirror. Her face felt unfamiliar, as if it belonged to someone else.

Father shouted from the living room, "She's what?" Chris cringed. Father was drunk, of course. He'd been drunk for months, gulping his government benefits for not working the farm. He wasn't used to not working. It was hard on him. "This wouldn't have happened if you'd had a boy!"

Mom murmured something, too soft for Chris to hear. Father screamed, "She got it from *your* grandmother! You take care of your freak child! I never would've married you if I'd thought this was going to happen!"

Chris turned away from the mirror and pulled the string for the light. She should be scrubbing the floor when Mom saw her again, or trying to wash the walls without tearing off yet another strip of cheap wallpaper. Mom had wanted new wallpaper for as long as Chris remembered, paper that didn't peel off the walls.

She snatched the bucket from under the sink and dropped it into the claw-foot iron bathtub. She would wash the floor; then Mom would see that she hadn't meant to be staring in the mirror, she'd only stopped on the way to get the bucket, she was responsible, really. She would ignore the fierce itching, the sudden urge to nibble on her lower lip.

She had just turned the clammy faucet for cold water when Mom reappeared in the doorway. "Chris, honey."

Chris turned to face her. *Don't frown, and don't smile.* If she smiled, Mom would think she was laughing at her.

"Why don't you go down to the basement and play for awhile?"

The basement had only one light bulb, dangling from the naked rafters, and smelled even more mildewy than the rest of the house. Spiders ruled most of it. Father sent her downstairs when she'd been bad.

Chris wanted to cry. "Okay."

Mom stepped back, watching Chris in the same way that she often looked at Dad. Chris didn't like it. She hadn't done anything. Why was Mom staring like that?

Chris walked past her mother, conscious of those eyes on her back. They went through the dusty family room, avoiding the doorway to the back room where Father sat in his big chair. She heard an aluminum can clatter; Father had thrown an empty beer can at the television.

"Dad's upset, just ignore him. I'll make you a couple sandwiches," Mom said quickly, softly. "Would you like some ham?"

Chris blinked. The ham was Father's. "I... is it okay?"

"Of course it's okay! I said you could, didn't I?"

"Thank you, Mom."

Chris' ragged sneakers always stuck to the kitchen tile, no matter how often she washed it. The table's bad leg was slightly askew again. She'd have to straighten it before it fell over and Mom and Dad yelled at her. She stood quietly by the basement door while Mom opened the fridge and took out a plastic bag of deli ham and a loaf of bread. When Mom quickly slapped three sandwiches together, with more ham and cheese than Dad ever got, Chris' eyes grew wide. And a pickle, too?

Mom wrapped everything in paper towels and shoved them in Chris' hands. "You go downstairs now, all right, honey?" Mom's smile was tight, and she kept glancing over her shoulder towards the back room.

Chris nodded. "All right, Mom."

Mom's smile relaxed a little, and she reached out as if to pat Chris' head. She jerked her hand back, however, and that careful look returned to her eyes. "Just you do as I say, and everything'll be okay." Mom said that at least once a day.

Chris walked down the stairs. The old wood creaked under her weight. When she was at the bottom and had pulled the string for the light, Mom pushed the door closed. Chris flinched when she heard the heavy deadbolt click into place.

"Hold it! Hold it, I said!" Father inhaled another mouthful of whiskey, picked up the black marker and turned to the gaping doorway.

Chris struggled to hold the four-inch square beam level as Father traced the ends on either side of the doorframe. He wanted to mount a heavy hinge on one side and a bracket on the other. Father said that when they finished, a bull could hit that door without making it quiver.

They had about four hours to get the new door installed. Maybe less.

The cracks in the irregular cinder-block walls made Chris shiver. They always looked like they were going to crash inwards in a flood of dirt and worms and something else, she didn't know what, but something filthy and with many teeth.

Chris' whole body had begun to itch, and she set the sandwiches down on the washtub to try to scratch her back. She couldn't reach the itch. Finally she picked up a twisted ruler from the concrete floor, checked it for anything crawling, and used it to claw between her shoulder blades.

But her legs itched too, and her arms, and her face, and even her tiny breasts. She scratched and scratched and abruptly found herself on the ground, scratching everywhere, twisting to touch all of herself at once. Her jaw began to hurt; she must have banged herself on the floor and not noticed. Her teeth ached, too.

The itching stopped suddenly, as if someone had thrown a switch. Chris sat up to catch her breath. Dad was shouting again. She could hear his voice through the floor, even though she didn't understand his words.

Mom cares about me, Chris thought. That's why she sent me downstairs and locked me in. Mom thought I'd be happier down here.

Dad cares, too. I know he does.

Lining one wall were rusty metal shelves covered with old bottles and books and parts of appliances that Father kept saying he'd fix. His big toolbox was a blocky shape beside the shelves. A narrow window faced east, just above ground level. From there, Chris could see the chicken coop, empty since a fox had taken them all. The sky was already turning dark blue with the coming night.

Night? Chris shivered. Mom didn't want her to stay down here all night, did she? She suddenly noticed the complex smells of mildew and rust blending together. They seemed stronger than they ever had before. There was no place to sit down, no place to get away from the spiders. She didn't see any spiders right now, but they would come out as soon as she relaxed.

The itching returned, even more strongly than before. Chris felt hair creeping out of her skin. She immediately forgot the spiders and fell down to scratch herself on the concrete floor. The bloated moon was low enough to fill the window, and seemed to be smiling at her.

Her jaw hurt even more. Her teeth abruptly felt sharp, then her shirt seemed to shrink and choke her, her pants twisted away from her skin, and the itch, the itch everywhere. She tore at her shirt, popping buttons, and finally ripped it off and flung it. The fur on her hands was gray now, and thicker, but she hardly noticed as she attacked her belt. The plastic threatened to cut her in half, and she scrabbled at the buckle with stubby fingers until it opened and she squeezed out of her pants.

Chris' hips had changed too, and they *hurt!* She rolled onto all fours, trying to get up, struggling to walk, quivering. She felt hot; she should have been sweating, but she wasn't.

⚜

Father wanted her to hold the crossbeam steady so he could drill guide holes for the screws. She understood, but the big piece of wood weighed more than she did and it shook horribly with the drill. Father didn't help; he was too intent on drilling as deep as he could, using hard shoves on the drill. Chris smelled burning insulation. Father didn't notice.

Yesterday, one of the boys at school had asked her to go to the spring dance with him. Her belly had burned at the thought, and she wanted to stammer "yes." Her skin had itched from underneath, though, and the night before, the moon had hung gibbous, so she'd said that she wouldn't be free tonight and turned away.

Chris held the wood as firmly as she could. Thankfully, it was steady enough.

The basement suddenly had become a lot less scary. The simple smells were a tapestry of sensation, telling her more than she ever thought possible. The concrete hurt her paws. Circling, she moved

47

like a race car, always hoping to find a way out of the hole, and never finding it.

The smell drifting through the windows, marking the fields and woods, maddened her and made her claw at the brick beneath the window. She wanted to leap up and squeeze through the tiny portal, but it was too high and too narrow.

When she tried clawing and scratching at the door, bits of the old wood broke away under her claws. She threw herself against the door repeatedly, but it only rattled in the doorframe.

The meat in the sandwiches tantalized her, but the smell of the processing made her turn away. She couldn't eat the pickle either, even though something in her remembered liking them.

She heard voices upstairs. Each word was distinct, but none meant anything. She barked for their attention. The voices stopped, then began again.

When Mom opened the door the next morning, Chris was naked, sleeping curled up on her clothes. For once, she didn't have to do her chores that day.

The new door was up. Four inches thick. Solid oak. The old deadbolt was uselessly warped, and the doorframe was cracked. Father had set the new hinge and latch in support beams to either side of the doorframe. The crossbeam stood upright on its hinge, ready to drop into the latch and bar the door. Chris had seen similar doors on TV, late at night. They kept all sorts of monsters out.

By the second month, a routine had been established. Hair grew on Chris' face and neck. Mom made her something to eat, and asked her to go downstairs. The deadbolt clicked.

Mom became thinner. Father became louder. Chris knew that he cared – he wouldn't yell if he didn't care – but she wished that he'd be nice, just once in a while.

In September, she had gone to school the day before the night. The other students laughed at the soft hair on her face and hands, and she was sent home early. Mom didn't ask why but stopped making her go to school when she didn't get out of bed.

On the days she stayed home from school, Father drank even more. He either mumbled at the floor or shouted for Chris to bring him another beer. His eyes were bloodshot and hard when she brought the sweating cans, and he stared coldly at her without saying anything.

It's my fault, Chris thought. Something's wrong with me.

Sometimes Chris dreamed of telling her father to be quiet, telling her mother that she wanted to go out under the moon. Father would have yelled at her, though, and Mom would have shaken her head and said, "You shouldn't," with a hint of tears. They knew what they were doing.

In the tenth grade, on her first day of woodworking class, Chris found herself staring at a razor knife in her hand. The fluorescent light glinted blue and white on the cutting edge, parallel to her bony fingers. It's wrong, she thought. It should rip, tear, not slice.

She shuddered. That afternoon, Chris quit the woodworking class and signed up for Modern English. At the end of the semester, she brought her report card home, covered with A's and a B. Father looked at the report card and said, "I thought you were taking woodworking? You signed up for woodworking, didn't you? Go to your room!"

Mom smiled thinly, and said that she'd done well. "Just ignore your father, he's had a bad day."

More and more often, Mom gave her those Father-looks. Chris began spending long hours walking through the fields and woods, looking at the wildlife and wondering what it would all smell like.

Circling in the basement, she had somehow remembered the sensation of opened arteries spilling into her mouth, the toughness of gristle in her teeth. She'd never had meat that fresh. Still, it seemed right. The moon shone through the window, and she wanted to run through the woods and play tag with it, find a good spot of ground to make her own and mark her fur with its scent.

She circled again and again, almost swallowing her own tail. Claws ticked on concrete. *The voices overhead hold me in this hole,* she thought. The scent of woods edged through the window. Splinters of door covered the stair.

They *still* wouldn't let her out.

The door was getting thin.

Father grabbed the crossbeam and dropped it into the U-shaped latch, then tugged on the handle with all his weight. The door didn't even rattle. "That'll hold."

You, Chris silently finished.

Father clenched his whiskey bottle and shuffled towards the front of the house. "Pick up the tools and put them downstairs."

The wrenches, hammers, and screwdrivers were scattered over half the kitchen, greasing the ancient tile. She'd have to wash the floor.

This door looked much more solid than the old one. Chris remembered gouging the door until her claws and teeth bled, until the door had been thin enough to punch a single claw through. She felt ill with disappointment. It was going to be worse tonight.

Chris threw a pair of wrenches into the toolbox. Father had gone through all of the screwdrivers before finding one that fit the screws on the bracket. She put the screwdrivers away one at a time, until she held the last one in her hand: the one Father had used to turn the four heavy screws into the beam. Father had tightened them so forcefully that the bracket had sunk into the wood.

Circling.

It wasn't right, holding something trapped.

Scratching.

With a trembling hand, Chris fumbled the screwdriver up to the bracket. One screw would hold it in place long enough to fool Father. Just one night, one night under the moon.

Biting.

Chris stopped, dimly remembering the taste of meat, the tear of a grisly throat. She couldn't... wouldn't...

Tears came to her eyes, and she blinked them away. She rubbed one side of her face with a grimy hand, then dropped the screwdriver into the toolbox. She crouched and grabbed the handle. The toolbox shifted, and she felt her back muscles tighten. She pulled harder, and one side of the box rose an inch.

She stood, looking at the stairs, then back towards the living room. "Father?"

"What?" he shouted.

"I've got a problem."

She heard a muffled curse, then his footsteps tromped closer. "What?" he asked as he came through the door.

"I picked up the tools, but I can't lift them."

"Goddamn girl," he growled, then snatched up the box with one hand. "You get something and clean up the floor."

She watched Father sidle down the stairs, moving heavily with the tools. Before she knew it, her hand had swung out and slammed the door. The other hand swung the crossbeam into place.

She still had time to wash the floor before the moon rose.

STICKY NOTES

If I'd had to guess which of my friends was most likely to put a double-barreled shotgun under his chin and blast out the top of his skull, I would have said Kevin. Seeing Kevin in a suit and tie instead of his usual black leather and shadowed eyes, standing silently by Pete's closed coffin, seemed an impossible reversal.

My eyes still burned from two days of cleaning Pete's apartment. Both my own grief and the thousand shocking surprises amidst the trash had kept tears flowing even when I'd thought them exhausted. Pete's mom Betty sat on a couch near the coffin, simultaneously dumpy and fragile, her brother and mother hovering nearby as if expecting her to collapse at any time. After all the antiseptic the cleaning crew had used, my nose had gone numb to the funeral home's underlying stink, but I knew it was there. A few other friends talked in small groups, either waiting their turn for a moment at the casket or recovering from one.

My wife Heather sat with our friend Sam at the back of the room, talking quietly, foreheads almost touching as they whispered beneath a flower wreath. Heather comes up to my chin, so thin and supple she could be a child, but I've always thought she was the most desirable woman I'd ever seen. And her heart was big enough for both of us.

I could get through this. I'd been through awful things before. My palms turned up so I could stare at the scars where my pinkie fingers had been. The scars were only visible because each side was a slightly different color and the lines in the skin didn't match up. I remembered being twelve years old and curled up in Uncle Dalton's spare bedroom, crying and doubled over, wadded tissue clenched between my buttocks to absorb the thin trickle of blood while Uncle Dalton hummed drunkenly in the living room. Had that been worse than this? Fifteen years had dulled the memory somewhat, but I didn't think so. Nothing was worse than these last two days.

"Pete is dead," his mother had said over the phone. "Can you come over to his place? He left us – you and me – a note."

Somehow the call from Betty hadn't shocked me. Pete had always had a dark streak, not like Kevin's romance with morbidity but a serious menace that lurked in his soul and occasionally echoed through his laugh and his gestures, like the dim shadow of a shark racing along the ocean floor. I was shaking so badly that Heather had to drive me out to Pete's apartment to meet Betty over the ruins of her son's life.

Pete's apartment door stood open when we arrived. Betty sat on the balcony with a photo album on her lap, staring sightlessly at the car park. I walked across the grass, habitually staying as far away as possible from the two preadolescent boys tossing a baseball in front of the apartment next door. "Hi, Betty. How are you?" *That's a stupid question, how do you think she is?*

Betty looked up at me, eyes blinking owlishly in her pale face. "Thanks for coming." Her breath sounded like a failing machine, punctuated by starts and stops and coughs.

"Of course," I said. "What... what happened?" Heather squeezed my hand.

Betty spoke in an emotionless monotone. "I hadn't heard from Pete all week. He wouldn't answer the phone. He always calls – *called* three times a week, even when he was out of town. He always answered his cell phone, too, or called me back right away. I don't like calling his cell. It costs too much. I came to see the manager. He sent the maintenance man over to check." Her hands fluttered uselessly, as if internal pressures made them flail but her brain wasn't involved. "I followed him over. He said he couldn't let me in, but he couldn't stop me from following him up the walk."

Betty's voice dropped, as if she spoke from the bottom of an empty well. "He unlocked the door and jumped back. Knocked me down. He was screaming 'Don't go in there!' over and over again. He locked the door before I could get up, and wouldn't tell me anything. He called the police right there, from his cell phone." She looked back at the photo album. "I'm afraid I hit him. He wouldn't give me the keys."

"I'm sorry," I said quietly. "It wasn't your fault."

"I wanted to see, but the police officer wouldn't let me." I had to lean close to hear her. "Shotgun. He used a shotgun. I'd had his fingerprints taken when he was a boy. That's how they made sure it was him."

Heather put an arm around Betty, and I put my hand on Betty's shoulder. Words are inadequate a lot of the time, but sometimes they're so flimsy that even silence is better.

Betty said "Pete left a note, for both of us." After a long ragged moment she said, "You can have anything that he didn't leave to someone else."

There didn't seem to be anything for it. I stepped through the open door.

Pete hadn't let me into his apartment in a couple years. "It's a mess," he'd say with a faint smile. "I'm a bachelor, there's never any reason to clean up. Why don't we meet at the Thai restaurant?" Our friendship was set in coffee houses, late-night donut shops, movie theaters showing art flicks and B movies by obscure directors we shared an interest in. Now, my nose wrinkled at the stench coming through Pete's open door: mold, dust, and far, far too much bleach.

As my eyes adjusted to the gloom, vague looming shadows resolved into towering shelves and piled boxes. Books, videos, and magazines overflowed the shelves, heaps as high as my waist that toppled into the middle of the living room floor. Novels of every genre, magazines from supermarket tabloids to hardcore pornography, collectible comic books, all reduced to compost. Various Crowley texts and a condensed Golden Bough sat in a neat stack beside the door. Narrow aisles, perhaps wide enough for one size 8 foot to follow another, led from the doorway towards the mound of trash bags filling the back of the living room. Printer paper lay scattered everywhere, ephemera printed off the Web and tossed aside but not discarded. The only clean spot I could see was the tiled entryway where I stood.

Too clean.

The floor had been freshly scrubbed, ammonia and bleach and some chemical deodorizer that burned my nose but didn't quite cover some darker stench. The walls were badly scratched, as if someone had worked them over with a stiff brush until the outer layer of paint had abraded away. Overhead, a random scatter of irregular holes pocked the ceiling. I frowned, puzzled, then the image came to me. A shotgun under the chin, fired straight up, bits of tooth and skull and brain hurtling skyward, some of it puncturing the drywall, some of it wedging into the airspace above the ceiling, most of it raining back to the floor as the ruins of a life.

That's when I sank to my knees, staring at the ceiling, my breath hissing out and not coming back, my arms folding over my gut as if I'd been sliced open and my heart and all the rest of my innards were about to spill out across the floor. Heather took me in her arms right there, held me against her, murmuring quiet meaningless words as the pain crashed through me.

We could stand there and stare at the mess, or we could do something. We cleaned.

As a freelance computer consultant, Pete had pounded through a keyboard every six months or so. I remember him griping about his problems finding keyboards with the right resistance and feel, the correct spacing of keys, the proper function buttons along the top, the Control and Caps Lock keys in the right places. I didn't realize that when a keyboard wore out he put it back in the original packaging and stashed it in a closet. He had fourteen worn-out keyboards stacked on top of a box of clothes he hadn't worn since high school.

He hadn't opened any mail this year. Collection notices, past due bills, and Internal Revenue notices lay intermingled with months of advertising circulars and catalogs in plain brown envelopes. The electricity was off.

Pete had left a suicide note on his pillow, addressed to Betty and myself. The short note just said that his debts had ruined his life, and asked us to offer his friends his personal belongings as he'd designated. He'd left me a stack of stuff he thought I'd enjoy, my choice of anything he hadn't given to anyone else, and "your heart's truest desire." Somehow, I didn't think he had that last.

The bed held piles of books, CDs, magazines, videos, and comic books, leaving just enough room for a person to sleep if he lay very still. Each pile had a yellow sticky note on top of it with someone's name. Similar piles sat on heaps of unwashed clothing, or on boxes of debris. Some had toppled, making them impossible to differentiate one from another or from the underlying kipple.

Worst of all, the cleaning crew hadn't found everything. I'd pick up an issue of the Journal of the Alchemical Society only to find a fragment of bloody skull or a piece of brain the size of my missing pinkies behind it. Flies were already settling in. I couldn't imagine this after a week, or two, and I couldn't conceive having the apartment clean in less than a month. I fled more than once, to lean over the flowerbed and let my already-empty stomach heave strings of acid bile onto the grass, shaking and crying and trying not to believe.

This morass wasn't really my problem, of course. The landlord could take a picture and share it with his fellow landlords: "Security deposit, worst-case scenario." But this debris was the outward manifestation of Pete's mind, the only record of his secret deterioration. We knew why Pete said he'd pulled the trigger, but something deep within whispered that a better explanation, the *true* explanation, lurked somewhere within the trash of his life.

You cannot make the best of turning over an anime video with a garishly colored alien raping a schoolgirl on the cover and finding a chunk of your best friend's jaw with a broken crown still attached, but you can still do what needs doing. That was one helpful lesson from my summer with Uncle Dalton. I'd called Mom after losing my right pinkie. She'd cried, and asked if I was all right. I'd begged to come home, to leave Uncle Dalton's farm and come home to Florida. She'd said "of course" and then asked to talk to Uncle Dalton. He said I'd be fine, and convinced her that I might as well finish out the summer like we'd all planned. She did fetch me halfway through August, after Uncle Dalton took the other pinkie. By then everything my uncle wanted to do to me, everything he wanted me to think was normal, was already wired into my brain.

There's no point in complaining, or crying, or asking for help, because when it's really bad nobody can help you. You just do what you must.

The pile of occult books near the door was only the leading edge of a collapsed stack. The cleaning crew had taken the top layer, but some prizes remained: the four-column Talmud in gold leaf, reams of occult magazines from the last hundred years, a Nag Hammadi Codex in the original Coptic with the modern translation on opposing pages. I scraped up the leading edge to reveal tiny symbols and lines painted on the floor.

Curiosity flickered, and I cleared away the slurry to uncover the whole design. Lines and symbols in red and blue paint, the largest the size of my thumbnail, covered the entryway floor beneath a slurry of occult desiderata. I recognized some of the symbols from the books I'd been stacking. Others looked mathematical, or like something from a physics textbook. Neither Heather nor Betty recognized any of it. They seemed arranged in a circle, one edge destroyed by the forensic cleanup company. Now that I looked, I saw flecks of red and blue embedded in the scrubbed linoleum as well. Lines swirled around everything, a spiral that narrowed down to a tight circle just a few inches across, the central symbols the size of an ant. The circle was exactly large enough to contain the glass sphere buried by the clutter.

The witch glass was a blue-green irregular sphere about the size of a large tomato, with strands of glass trailing through the hollow center. Glassblowers' discards used hundreds of years ago as traps for roaming spirits, today they were tourist kitsch. This one had yet another yellow sticky note taped to it, labeled in Pete's draftsman printing "Your Heart's Truest Desire." I picked it up, and it flashed in the sunlight coming through the door.

Heather drove me back to our trailer that evening, a box of books bearing my name in the back seat. I cradled the witch glass in my left hand the whole way home, staring into it thoughtlessly. She put me in the shower, the box of books in the library, and the witch glass on a bookshelf, before feeding me a supper of tranquilizers with a side of soup.

The funeral was a sham.

Pete had ordered prepaid funeral services the month before, using a charge card that was well over its limit. The funeral home didn't want to honor the agreement, but Betty declared that Pete would have the simple service and cremation he had desired and paid the contract. The rent-a-reverend offered textbook prayers and a generic eulogy, carefully failing to mention that Pete was a suicide and hence destined for Hell no matter how fiercely we prayed. Heather held my hand, or sat close as I clutched her arm. Everyone watched solemnly as the minister offered the last prayer, thanked us for coming, and turned to leave.

The tension in the room snapped like punctured glass. Bright conversation flared here and there amid shards of solemnity. People smiled, shaking hands with those around them. It felt wrong. Someone laughed, as if hearing a good joke. A friend's casket dominated one end of the room, a friend who had destroyed himself so thoroughly that none of us could open the casket to say goodbye, and nobody had mentioned that little detail during the service?

My bowels churned as if I'd swallowed a live snake, and abruptly everyone changed. Their skin turned transparent, revealing the gears within, the wiring that transmitted orders through the body and the motors that powered their limbs. A bent old man at the end of the aisle had a corroded skeleton, bolts and rivets and girders rusted and twisted over decades, gap-toothed gears catching as he tried to raise an arm to shake someone else's spring-driven hand. The pregnant woman at the front of the room had a rolling, twisting assembly process within her bulging abdomen, cranes swiveling and mechanical riveters assembling next year's model. Understanding came immediately; everyone had changed their attitude because the cams and gears driving them said it was time to do so.

The springs along Heather's temple pulled to mimic a furrowed brow. "What's wrong?" came from a circular speaker in her throat, wired to an old-fashioned reel-to-reel recorder where her lungs should have been.

"This isn't happening," I whispered, staring around the room. A terrifying compulsion to look at my own hands washed over me, a sickening urge I didn't dare indulge. As my chin unwillingly dropped I squeezed my eyes shut. My hands clenched into fists, but the touch of bronze fingertips on my palms made them spasm open again, fingers spread to not touch each other. Heather took my arm with her cold mechanical hands, steering me from the room. Something else gripped my left side, murmuring quietly as we shuffled through the door and into the night.

The street was no better. The streetlights cast pools of acid light that stripped away every facade. Automobiles growled, wild beasts barely controlled by the machines behind the wheel. A stench of blood and grease clotted in my throat. Trees fluttered in the breeze, bronze leaves clattering against iron bark.

Stumbling and shuffling, I was turned towards the end of the block. Cable-driven hands urged me to walk. "It's all right," said Heather, the faint static of a recording hissing behind every word. "It'll be all right."

At the end of the block, something moved overhead. I lifted my head to see a figure drifting in midair between the trees. Its bones were hollow aluminum, like a lawnchair, and the tiny gears and pulleys within whirred like clockwork. The central flywheel spun frantically to power the wings of mesh and plastic that buzzed back and forth as it regarded me.

I squeezed my eyes shut. "No. This isn't real."

Just like that Heather's hand on my arm became warm and soft, the trees rustled instead of rattling. I took a shaking breath and stopped walking.

"Are you all right?" my friend Derek asked, his muscled arms and red hair now visible.

"Yeah." I took another deep breath, turning. Heather held my other arm, nothing but concern on her face, pale skin once again concealing the mysteries beneath.

Riding home afterwards, I thought the explanation was simple. We can only handle so much sorrow, and Pete's friends and family were just waiting for someone to say "It's all right, grieving time is done" to rest their pain for a time. Spending two days cleaning out the apartment, never knowing where something especially ghastly lurked, had stretched my emotions like a rubber band extended too far for too long. I just needed a break. Nothing to really worry about.

We made love fiercely that night, affirming life the best way we knew how. Afterwards we lay side by side, gazing into each other's eyes, silently cradling and prolonging our intimacy. My hand stroked up and down her flank. Heather is small, thin, her hips narrow, her breasts no more than an A cup. She smiled sleepily. "Love you." Her tiny hand rested on the back of my head.

"I love you too." I treasure Heather. I'm not sure I can really, truly love anyone, not the way people talk about it, but she is unquestionably the best person I know.

"It's going to be all right."

"I know." I lightly kissed her nose. "It'll take time." My fingertips circled her small buttocks. "I'm sorry about all this."

"It's not your fault." Her voice wasn't even a whisper, more the sound she made as she gently exhaled.

"No, it's not."

We were silent for a moment, then she said "You love me even if I can't have children?"

I smiled. "I married you to be with you, remember? I don't need to have kids." When I asked Heather to marry me I decided I'd take her love, and return what I passed off as love in exchange. It was fraud, but honest fraud, best-effort fraud. And all anyone can offer is their best effort.

My hand reached around behind her, lightly stroking her inner thigh. She smiled sleepily. "Don't start anything you can't finish."

I moved closer and kissed her again, then wrapped my arms around her and pulled her body against mine. *She's so small, it's like she never grew up.* My heart beat faster.

Afterwards I got up to use the bathroom. As I padded back down the hall, something glistened and sparked in the darkened library. I stopped and peered.

The witch glass on the library shelf gleamed and flickered, then turned dark again.

I shook my head. Just a reflection, some stray headlight off the street seeping through a crack in the blinds.

Heather was asleep when I crawled back into bed, but when I touched her hand she smiled and tangled her fingers with mine. I'll never tell her how grateful I am that she can't have children. She might ask me why.

✸

Of course, Betty and I gave up. There was too much debris, and no real answer. I'd burned up half my vacation time crawling halfway through the apartment, and Betty's job paid hourly. We wound up picking through the pile to salvage things of obvious value and telling the landlord to get rid of the rest. When we left he was telling the contractor to replace every piece of drywall and insulation in the entryway and to clear out the trash. I told Betty to call if she needed me, and walked away without looking back.

Going back to work at the bookstore the next day was a relief. I might just be a flunky at this big chain store, but after the last few days there was a quiet satisfaction in reading the shelves of the history and computer science sections, ensuring every book was in order. The most horrifying thing I found was a Dean Koontz novel filed under "Operating Systems." I had to sub at the cash register during lunch, but other than that I was left to my peaceful, meditative task. My coworkers knew what had happened, knew it had been bad even if they couldn't understand just how horrific. I stopped on the way home and bought a bouquet of flowers and a bar of nice chocolate for Heather, small thanks for all she'd done but enough to show my appreciation.

And so life veered back towards normal.

Kevin invited us over to his place for pizza and cards with a bunch of friends that that Friday evening. The word he didn't use was "wake," but we knew exactly what he meant. By ten o'clock a dozen of us sat in a rough circle around the living room, empty pizza boxes in the corner, the cards and games forgotten on the kitchen

61

table, drinks in hand. Heather had a beer, while I had a cola. Nobody could blame me for getting puke-in-the-bushes drunk tonight, but the mere aroma of whiskey resurrected fifteen-year-old memories. No amount of toothpaste or mouthwash could erase the taste, but whiskey had scorched it away. Uncle Dalton gave me anything I wanted, once I gave him everything he wanted. Even thinking of getting drunk felt like unlocking a door that I'd spent fifteen years barricading.

We talked freely, and then a slow silence seeped into the room. Sam eventually said "You know, right about now Pete would say something outrageous. We need another way to jump-start conversations."

"Yeah, he was good at that," Kevin said, taking another swallow of hard cider. He wore blue jeans and a white T-shirt, as if Pete's death had slapped the goth out of him. "You could always count on Pete to start an argument that would run all night. Remember 'good art makes you feel molested?'"

"I still can't believe he's gone," said Karen.

I lifted my glass. "To Pete, the damned fool. May the first of us to figure out how to raise the dead let the rest of us know so we can line up to kick his ass." Glasses and bottles clinked.

Sam said, "What could make someone do that?"

You read the note, you twit. That's all there is to know. "He felt trapped," I said. "No way out. Ruined."

"He had a good business," said someone behind me.

"And he spent it all on books, and music." I took another swallow of cola, wishing that I dared something stronger. "He tried to absorb everything, and couldn't."

"There wasn't anything else in the apartment?" asked Kevin.

I shook my head. "There was everything else in the apartment. I had no idea he had so much junk. If he'd let me in, I would have seen. If he'd let any of us in, we would have seen. We would have known he wasn't right."

"Schizo-affective disorder," said Jim slowly. "Looking back, it fits."

"You're the med student," said Karen sharply. "Couldn't you have seen that earlier?"

Jim shook his head. "Most schizo-affectives are terribly smart — geniuses, who know something's not right, and they're paranoid enough to not be caught."

"We all know Pete wasn't right," laughed Kevin hollowly.

"But where's the line between 'odd duck' and 'crazy'?" said Fred, his first words in an hour. "If they could lock you up for being weird, Kevin would have spent his life in the extra-padded room." That got more of a laugh then it deserved.

Jim said "I think that the important thing is, there's always a better way out. For everyone. Even if you can't see it. If anyone in this room has problems, now or whenever, remember that you have friends." His gaze passed around the room, locking eyes with each of us. "We'll help each other. Talk to someone before it's too late. I don't care what you've done, what kind of hole you're in, I'll help you. Even if you piss me off, I'll help you."

Kevin raised his glass. "Remember that, guys. We're all here for each other. You're all good people. Even Fred."

I raised my glass, making the appropriate noises. All good people? If you knew what I really was, you'd burn me at the stake. And I'm only a good person because I choose to be. I make that choice every day, every single minute.

As the party fractured I walked people out, handing each a bundle from the back of our car. Books, magazines, comics, music, all bound with twine, each labeled in Pete's clear handwriting.

I drove home quietly, Heather slightly buzzed in the passenger seat. I didn't begrudge her that escape – if I'd had a bad week mourning my friend, she'd had a bad week watching her husband disintegrate. We were pulling in the driveway when she said "You know, you can tell me anything."

"I know that."

"I'd love you just the same."

"I'd love you just the same, too. No matter what." She really could tell me anything, I realized. For a liberating moment I considered actually telling her, unburdening myself of my worst desires, but the mere thought brought a flash of pain to my hands and I heard Uncle Dalton screaming "Here's for tattletales!" over the chainsaw's roar, my hand duct-taped to a plank, the pinkie curled helpless over the edge of the board. There's nothing anyone can do, no medication that can change me, no catharsis can purge me clean. All I can do is not be myself, not be a twenty-first-century Uncle Dalton.

Heather slipped off for a quick shower before bed, and I stripped to my boxers and meandered around the trailer waiting for my turn. I imagined my friends taking their bundles home, little stacks of knowledge that Pete had thought each would find most interesting or valuable. What did they say about what Pete thought about each of them? That's when I realized that I had never looked at the stack with my name on it.

I walked to the library. The breeze had pushed the door shut, but the latch never works on that door anyway. I reached to push it open, and my hand sank right through the wood and vanished up to the forearm.

Recoiling I hit the opposite wall with my bare back, clutching one hand with the other and staring at the door as if it had grown fangs, my heart bludgeoning my ribs. Heather sang tunelessly in the shower. My heart gradually slowed as I stared at my hand, and I began to think more clearly. It had been a long week. Surely it had been some trick of perspective and fatigue, the dark wood and the shadows of the dimly-lit hall. You cannot reach through a closed door.

I needed some time away. A few days without any responsibilities, to the dead or the living.

This time, the door opened at my touch. Our books sat in neat rows on stained and varnished pine shelves built into the walls, fiction alphabetical by author, nonfiction by subject. A floor lamp and a comfortable chair sat in the middle of the floor, and a small leather couch slouched beneath the window, the colors blending nicely with the thickly padded shag carpet that was a delight to every step. Pete's legacy sat beside the reading chair in a corrugated cardboard box: two graphic novels from a Japanese company I'd never heard of, in French. Two Phil Dick hardcovers and one J. G. Ballard softcover, all yellow with age. A handful of CDs from Nurse With Wound and Sigue Sigue Sputnik. Beneath those sat a trade paperback of Baudelaire's *Fleurs du Mal*, a yellow bookmark sticking out the top. I frowned. Had Pete marked a passage for me, left a private explanation? The paper wouldn't come out – it was yet another sticky note. I opened to the page and saw his writing on the bookmark.

For my best friend,
Be sure to ask the coroner about my last sick practical joke.
—Pete

The scream tore out of me like water from a bursting balloon, leaving nothing inside except more screams. After the second I crammed my fist into my mouth, biting down on the space between my thumb and first finger, the pain in my hand not quite a distraction from the agony in my heart.

Heather came running from the bathroom, dripping soap, her hair plastered against her head. "What is it?"

I couldn't speak, just held out the book mutely, the space marked with my thumb. Heather took it, glanced at the note, and threw the book aside. "It's all right," she said, one hand on my back, the other gently urging my clenched fist out from my teeth, stroking and soothing with a wet touch. "Don't look at those. I'll check them for you, make sure they're all right. You don't need to look. It's all right."

It was a long moment before I could unclench my fist and put that hand around her, heedless of the blood dripping from my hand and running down her wet back. My mind had shut down. There was nothing more to think.

On the shelf behind Heather the witch glass shone with inner light, rays of blue and gold piercing my eyes. I didn't think anything of that at the time, any more than I thought of my naked soapy wife dripping on the carpet or the hollowness in my chest.

Some time later I was able to whisper, "I'm sorry."

"I hate him," Heather said quietly to my chest.

"What?"

She looked up into my eyes. "For what Pete did. For what he's done to you. I hate him. It's horrible."

"He." My thoughts were only beginning to fire again. "He was hurting. Ill."

She nodded at the book tossed into the corner. "*That's* hurting. That's hurtful, and ill, and sick, cruel, vile. That goddamn sick son-of-a-bitch."

"He was my friend."

"He was *your* friend. I got him when I married you, part of the package. And someone needs to tell you. He was sick. Sick, sick sick."

I only blinked.

She sighed and stroked my hair. "I know it's hard. But don't let him take you down too, all right? If you need to talk to someone, I'm here. If you need someone to listen professionally I mean, I'll set it up. There's no shame in that."

The light in the witch glass flickered and dissipated. "I'm all right," I said. "It's hard. But I have you."

"You do have me." She didn't smile. "Remember that."

"I will."

She squeezed me tighter. "Come on," she said. "Let's clean up your hand."

I couldn't help noticing as we walked back that she seemed even thinner than usual, the gentle curve of her hips less pronounced, her walk more level. I blinked, but the image persisted all through the night.

I have enough seniority to not work Saturday, but after missing all those days I had volunteered to pick up the closing shift from one of the guys who had filled in for me earlier. I woke up at nine, three hours before I started, and made Heather breakfast in bed before she went to her mother's. We were just finishing when the doorbell rang.

"I'll get it," I said, pulling on a sweatsuit. "You relax."

I opened the door to find a boy, maybe eleven or twelve, in jeans and heavy work gloves, and flinched inwardly at the sight. "Hi, I'm Andy from across the street." His voice had the squeak of a boy just a few months short of adolescence.

"I know who you are," I said.

"My Hapkido dojo has been invited to Korea to participate in the world trials," he said. "We've had fundraisers, but I'm trying to raise money for myself, spending money for the trip. Do you need your lawn mowed, or any work around the house?"

66

"Sorry, kid," I said roughly. "Good luck, but I'm all set here." My lawn needed mowing, but I'd rather do it myself. I'd rather hire a lawn service. I'd rather hire an epileptic grandmother with a missing leg to mow my lawn than have anything to do with any boy the same age I had been.

"Come on, mister," he said. "Surely you have something than needs attention. Something I can do. I work hard, and I'll do anything." He looked me in the eye. "Anything at all."

I slammed the door in his face, and Andy said a word he shouldn't know at his age. I kept my back against the door until I heard him leave.

On my way back to the bedroom, I glanced into the library. The witch glass burned amber.

"Who was it?" Heather called.

"Just a kid looking for work." I stepped into the library, watching the orb. The light spun and quivered inside, no discernible source for its radiance. I picked it up, and the cool light chilled my palm.

Just as quickly as it appeared, the light went out.

I put the witch glass back on the shelf and went back to kiss my wife, get some real pants on, and mow my own lawn before work.

The Saturday customers aren't that different from the weekday crowd; a few make hit-and-run strikes for a particular title, but most just wander the aisles of their favorite section looking for something that sparks a whim. I manage the computer science, history, and literature sections, areas where the crowd is mostly college age and older. Today, though, my area seemed full of young boys. One looked at me curiously, and the world flashed like a photographic negative. I grabbed a shelf to regain my balance, blinking, and when my vision cleared the young man was smiling at me.

Once is something you ignore. Twice might be coincidence.

But when the color bled out the third time, and the young man in my section looked smiled and walked towards me, I knew something was shoving them at me. This was no illusion, no trick of perspective. It wasn't stress, unless it was the sort that bursts blood vessels in the brain. I spent ten minutes locked into a bathroom stall, forcing myself to breathe deeply and regularly to regain my self-control, then decided I'd take my break and walk around the store once or twice to burn off some of the frenetic energy possessing me.

Just outside the door, lost in my own thoughts, I almost didn't stop when someone called my name. I looked, and almost coughed up a lung.

"How's it going?" the man said.

"Pete?"

"It's the end of the month," Pete said. "I thought I'd come by, see how much of my book allowance you guys could soak up."

My mouth flapped uselessly.

His eyes narrowed. "Are you all right? I mean, you don't look good."

"Yeah," I managed. "I think I'm ill." I took a step back, then another.

"Maybe you should go home." He moved closer. I retreated again, my back hitting the door. "You're turning green. Sit down. I'll get help."

"No, that's OK. I have… errands."

"Errands can wait. You want me to call Heather? I can take you home."

"No," was all I could manage.

"Look, at least sit down," he said.

I fumbled my way to a bench and collapsed. "I'll be fine."

"Listen," he said, "I'm going inside for a minute. Don't go anywhere, all right?"

I must have nodded. Everything spun sickeningly, the world a whirligig carnival ride operated by a methamphetamine junkie.

Pete came out seconds later, trailing my manager. Jessica glanced at me and said, "That's it. You said you were well, you aren't. I know you're worried about your job, but don't. You're not faking being ill, you're faking being all right. I don't want to see you back without a doctor's note."

"Fine." I stared at Pete, a ball of vomit tight in my gut.

"I'll make sure he gets home all right," Pete said, sitting beside me.

"Thanks." Jessica went back inside, already thinking about how to rearrange the schedule for the next few days.

I was afraid to ask the next question. "Pete... can you afford books?"

He laughed. "You must be sick. I'm the Dollar Nazi, remember? So much each month for taxes, so much for rent, so much for books, so much for dining out."

"Right." Pete patted my shoulder, and the world lurched.

I closed my eyes and took a deep breath, exhaling fully, visualizing the shock flowing out of my lungs and fresh clean air coming in. "Listen. Pete. I'll be fine to drive home." I made myself speak clearly and slowly. "You get on with your day. I just needed to sit for a moment, that's all."

He studied my face. "All right. When you're up for it, there's a new noodle shop out by my place. I'll wait to try it until you're feeling better."

I was proud of myself; my voice didn't even shake as I said, "That would be great." Without another word, I walked away.

If I was crazy or ill, someone would notice. Pete had noticed, but I didn't think he counted. Heather deserved better, but if I had really snapped, she'd get me the help I needed.

Pete and I had talked about magic, many times. I'd had an idle interest back in college, and had finally given it up as self-delusion. Pete had a deeper interest, but he had a deeper interest in everything. I remembered that sacrifices drove the earliest magic, and the most potent sacrifices were human beings. The cleaning crew had scrubbed away the edge of the magic circle where I'd found the witch glass, I had to wonder: had it not been a circle, but two? Had Pete been standing within one when he pulled the trigger? If human sacrifice was magical power, just how strong was self-destruction? What could a sorcerer do if he really put his soul into something, if he really gave it everything he was? Had Pete created true magic, thinking that I would restore him? That I'd restore him as he wished to be, as I wished he'd been? He didn't know my secrets — *I* hardly knew my secrets.

Just what did I have? And how would I endure?

I wiped my sweaty palms on my pants and started the car. I needed to be home. Jessica was right, I was sick.

Streaks of yellow and red pulsed across the sky as I pulled up in front of our trailer. I blinked, but they remained for a dozen heartbeats before fading. Something told me that the witch glass shone those same colors at that very moment. I fumbled with the car door and staggered into the trailer.

Our home had changed.

It was our couch, and our kitchenette table, but different wallpaper. Our inherited nineteen-inch television had become a four-foot flat plasma humming like an entertainment Lamborghini. The pressed-board china cabinet remained, but instead of the Salvation Army plates we had gleaming porcelain. The faint aroma of prefabricated housing was gone, replaced with subtle scents of lavender and rose.

The tiny bunch of flowers I'd brought Heather were replaced by a booming rose bouquet, each flower the size of a fist.

I picked up a magazine on the coffee table. My name was on the subscription label.

What did I have? And what did I want? What was my "heart's truest desire?" The answer that kept bobbing to the top of my mind sickened me.

The library had changed as well, the thick soft carpet replaced by a polished wood floor. The witch glass shone neon on the library shelf, strobing from blue to yellow to red and back.

All I've ever wanted, my truest desire, was to be loved and accepted for who and what I am. I picked up the witch glass, its cold stinging my palm and settling deep into my hand, an ache like hypothermia creeping up my arm. What did I really want? Would the world, and everyone in it, keep changing until they met my wants?

"Are you all right?" someone said from the doorway.

I whirled. Heather stood there, almost.

The person had her face, but with hair cropped almost to the scalp. The eyes were hers, and the cheekbones, but the lips a little thinner.

The jacket I'd bought her, the one with her name embroidered onto the pocket, now said "Harry." Her breasts were gone. Those were pectoral muscles. And fifteen years had dropped away with the breasts.

I stared at Harry's face. Heather loved me, and I had no doubt that Harry did as well. Maybe even more so.

My legs buckled, and I sank to my knees.

I'd never have to tell anyone anything. Everything would be in place. Adoption or guardianship papers. School records all in order. And a young healthy boy wouldn't need to see the doctor often at all.

Pete's last note flashed across my brain. Heather had been right, that had been left to hurt me. Just because you love someone doesn't mean that you don't want to hurt them too. Just because you want something badly doesn't mean that you don't want it to *not* happen almost as badly.

I'm not sure I know what love is. But I knew that Heather loved me, just as she was. And I knew what that was worth.

With a horrid scream I raised the witch glass over my head and brought it down, twisting my body for extra strength, smashing it into the wooden floor. I felt rather than heard the crunch. Broken glass punctured my hand, driving through muscles and between bones, my lungs too empty to scream again. Somewhere in the distance, from a direction I can't point, Pete's faint wail echoed and faded forever.

I fell back onto the carpet, the blessed familiar shag carpet that Heather and I had picked out for this room, gasping, cradling the back of my lacerated hand, staring at the spikes of glass sticking out from the palm. Heather dashed forward, catching me as I fell, easing me back and crying out in pain as bad as my own.

I am not good.

I am not strong.

But with her, I am strong enough to never have what I want most.

ABOUT THE AUTHOR

https://mwl.io

Never miss another new release! Sign up for MWL's mailing list at https://mwl.io.

NOVELS AND COLLECTIONS (AS MICHAEL WARREN LUCAS):

Immortal Clay – Kipuka Blues

Butterfly Stomp Waltz – Terrapin Sky Tango

Forever Falls – Hydrogen Sleets – Drinking Heavy Water

$ git commit murder – $ git sync murder

Prohibition Orcs (coming 2022)

NONFICTION (AS MICHAEL W LUCAS):

Cash Flow for Creators – Relayd and Httpd Mastery

PAM Mastery – FreeBSD Mastery: Advanced ZFS

FreeBSD Mastery: Specialty Filesystems – FreeBSD Mastery: ZFS

Tarsnap Mastery – Networking for Systems Administrators

FreeBSD Mastery: Storage Essentials – Sudo Mastery

DNSSEC Mastery – Absolute OpenBSD – SSH Mastery

Network Flow Analysis – Absolute FreeBSD – PGP & GPG

Cisco Routers for the Desperate –FreeBSD Mastery: Jails

Ed Mastery – SNMP Mastery – TLS Mastery

The Networknomicon

Only Footnotes

See your favorite bookstore for more!